PLAYING TO WIN

The Trouble with Tomboys # 2

STEPHANIE STREET

PROLOGUE

Two years ago . . .

One three-week summer sports camp shouldn't have spawned such a tight knit friendship—but it did. Camp Haversham in Upstate New York was where Hannah, Jordan, and Alex met during the summer before their freshman year. Like most of the young athletes who'd flocked to the training camp, they hailed from different towns and schools. They might never have met if it hadn't been for Camp Haversham, and they definitely wouldn't have formed their little "Tomboy Trio" if it hadn't been for one brainless moron by the name of Noah Ackerbaum.

Noah and his crew were an obnoxious group of alphaholes who paraded around the grounds like they owned the place. Were they skilled at their respective sports? Yes. No one would deny that.

But these girls were better.

Noah and his minions were nice to the girls at the camp—particularly the hot girls—but for the most part, boys played boys and girls played girls.

Until they didn't.

That was Alex's fault. A phenom with the bat, the daughter of a professional baseball player hadn't loved the idea of being segregated. She wanted to play the best—whatever gender that might be.

After Jordan kicked Noah's butt in touch football, and Hannah took him down in soccer, it was Alex who decided they ought to have a soccer scrimmage that was boys versus girls. Noah begrudgingly agreed. From the way he'd talked it was like they were still in elementary school and kids actually used phrases like "you throw like a girl" as if that were a *bad* thing.

Lame.

Led by the three top female athletes at camp, the girls' team totally trounced the boys' team in a humiliating defeat.

Well, it probably wouldn't have been quite so humiliating if the losers hadn't been such poor sports about it.

Hannah was putting away her equipment when Noah entered the gymnasium behind her. "We let you win, you know that, right?"

She straightened, her dark brown ponytail swinging over her shoulder as she turned to face Noah. Two of his friends had come up behind him and were snickering—a dead giveaway that Noah was going into full bully mode.

Anyone who'd ever seen any movie set in a high school knew how to spot a bully a mile away, and Noah fit the part to a tee. Tall and handsome, he might have been charming if he had any sense of humility or dignity. As it was, he was petty and crass, his sense of humor having peaked at pranks and poop jokes.

"Excuse me?" Hannah said politely. She wasn't afraid of these guys, but she wouldn't deny that she was relieved to see her new friends trailing in behind Noah and his gang.

"What's going on here?" Alex asked. The tall, lean brunette stepped between Hannah and the boys, her shoulders back as her chin held high.

Jordan looked between Noah and the other girls warily before hurrying over to stand on Hannah's other side. "You okay?" she asked Hannah under her breath. The blonde was pretty in a very girlie sort of way, almost . . . dainty. One would never guess that she rocked it on the hockey rink.

"I'm fine," Hannah said, not bothering to lower her voice. She waved a hand toward the guys. "Noah here was just about to explain how they let us win." She couldn't quite hide the amusement in her voice . . . and truth be told, she didn't really try.

Alex gave a little huff of amusement as well. "Oh yeah? This ought to be good."

"You're girls," Noah said.

"Way to state the obvious," Alex replied.

"We'd get in trouble if we hurt you," one of the guys behind Noah added.

"Oh, I see," Hannah said. "So that's why you lost. You were being chivalrous and trying not to hurt us."

Even Jordan was laughing now, the idea so ludicrous. They'd all been out there on that field. No one had played dirtier than Noah.

"Really?" Alex said. "Is that what you think happened?"

Noah held his hands up, his head falling to the side with smarmy smirk that made the girls' skin crawl. "Hey, you guys go ahead and celebrate your little victory. But I thought you should know the truth."

"Uh huh," Hannah said. "And what truth is that? That we wiped the field with your butts?"

Alex snickered. "Or that you got beat by a bunch of girls?"

Noah's nostrils flared and his friends exchanged looks. "You know the trouble with tomboys?"

"No, please tell us," Alex said in a flat tone that made Hannah and Jordan snort with laughter.

"You're a bunch of freaks," he said. "Good luck finding a guy to date you."

Eye rolls all around.

"Thanks for the advice," Alex said. "But if you're referring to guys like you then I think I can speak for my friends here when I say we're better off single."

Noah huffed. "You couldn't get a date if your life depended on it."

"That's an interesting theory," Hannah said, her eyes narrowed as if giving it some serious thought. "I'll have to ask my *boyfriend* what he thinks about that."

Noah looked disgusted by their amusement, but at least he and his friends were backing away. He sneered at Hannah. "As if we'd believe any guy would be into *that*. You look like my little brother."

Hannah didn't seem to mind the insult, but Jordan stiffened at her side.

Alex narrowed her eyes on him. "Get out of here, losers."

Noah scoffed as he turned to go. "Whatever. We all know we handed you that win."

Jordan surprised them all by speaking up. "Then I guess you wouldn't mind a rematch?"

Noah turned back, staring at her as if she'd just sprouted another head. "What?"

She took a step forward, her arms crossed over her chest. "I said, if you're so sure we didn't win fair and square, maybe we should have another go. The three of us versus the three of you."

Noah's brows drew together and he stared at her like she was nuts, but he didn't respond.

Alex arched her brows. "What's the matter, boys? You scared you'll lose again?"

They laughed until the boys were gone. They didn't stop laughing until they'd put away the rest of the equipment and were heading back to the girls' dorm to shower.

"Thanks for having my back," Hannah said.

"What are fellow tomboys for?" Alex said, slinging an arm around her shoulders.

Jordan dropped her voice in a terrible impression. "You know the trouble with tomboys . . ."

They all cracked up.

"What a moron," Hannah said.

"I'm so glad you stood up to him, Alex," Jordan added.

Alex hitched her hip to bump Jordan, who was walking on her other side. "And *you*. I can't believe you outright challenged him to a rematch."

Hannah leaned forward to grin at the blonde. "Seriously. Mad props, girl."

Jordan clapped a hand over her mouth and shook her head. When she dropped her hand, she said, "Honestly? I can't believe I did that either." She turned to Hannah. "But what about you? '*I'll have to ask my boyfriend . . .!*'"

Alex laughed. "That was awesome. His face was priceless." She looked down at Hannah. "Were you making that up?"

Hannah shook her head. "No, I really do have a boyfriend. We've been together since middle school."

"Wow," Alex said. "Since *middle school?*"

"He's on my intramural soccer team," Hannah said, as though that explained anything.

"He plays for your *team?*" Jordan sounded alarmed. "Aren't you worried about messing up the team if something happens?"

Hannah shook her head. "Not really. I mean, we've been friends forever, and we're not one of the dramatic couples who are into PDA or big fights or anything. We just . . . get along well."

Alex feigned a yawn. "Wow, that sounds really . . . romantic."

Jordan laughed as Hannah shrugged again. "It works for us. What about you guys? Any boyfriends? Crushes?"

The answer was a unanimous 'nah.' Neither seemed terribly put out about it.

"What a dumb insult," Alex said. She tossed her hair back over her shoulder. "As if I couldn't get a boyfriend if I wanted one."

"Seriously," Hannah agreed. "As if any of us are desperate for a guy."

Jordan laughed. "I mean, we've got more important things to worry about, like school and our teams. Who even has time for a relationship?"

After a brief silence, Alex made a bold statement. "Noah is an idiot."

"Agreed," Jordan said.

Hannah leaned forward to look at the other two. "You know the *real* trouble with tomboys?"

Alex arched a brow, a twinkle in her eyes. "They're afraid of us."

Jordan laughed, "Exactly."

CHAPTER ONE

Jordan

Hannah: Good luck on your first day of school!
   Me: Thanks. I'm more worried about hockey.
   Alex: Don't sweat it. You got this.
   Hannah: You're awesome. Don't forget it.

Best friends were a girl's lifeblood, right? I didn't know what I'd do without mine. We had to work a little harder than most to stay in touch since we lived in different states, but that was okay. I knew no matter what, Hannah and Alex had my back. I could tell them anything, and they'd understand.

This was why I texted them as soon as I found out I'd made it onto the boys' hockey team. Hannah played intramural soccer on a co-ed team, so she had a lot of great advice about dealing with the guys on my team. But even she'd never been the only girl on an all-boys team before.

Like Alex, I had a lot of brothers, so dealing with dumb guys wasn't a completely foreign concept, but still. I was nervous.

   Me: As long as I remember Rule #1, I'll be just fine.

Alex: *groan*

Hannah: Here we go...

Me: Hey! Some of us *cough, Hannah* would have fewer problems right now if they stuck to The Rule.

Hannah: Don't bring me into this. I'm doing just fine.

Alex: As much as I love you guys, gotta go. Some of us have been in school for a week already and have a bunch of junk to do.

Hannah: Yeah, I have to go, too. Seriously, Jord, don't stress. Everything will be amazing. You will be amazing.

Me: Thanks. You guys are the best! TTYL

Talking to my camp besties was just what I needed. Not that Alex and Hannah were my only friends, they just offered an outside opinion when I needed one. And after our experience at Camp Haversham, I knew they understood what it was like to compete with boys.

"You ready, Jordan!" My younger brother, Payton, shouted up the stairs.

"Just a sec!" I shouted back, taking one last look in the mirror. I dressed like a tomboy, no denying it, but I wasn't built like one, for sure. With long blonde hair and an hourglass figure, no one could mistake me for a boy even in all my hockey gear. There would be no hiding my obvious female attributes on the all-male hockey team. And starting that afternoon, right after school, I'd get a solid look at being the only girl on the ice.

I fluffed my blonde curls one last time and headed down the stairs.

Payton waited, impatiently shifting from one foot to the other, holding a duffle bag and a hockey stick. Mine were already in the trunk of my car.

"Okay, let's go."

For all his fidgeting, Payton was in no hurry out the door to the beat-up car sitting in our driveway. I'd inherited it from my older brother, Joe, when he moved out last year. Before that, it belonged to our oldest brother, Bobby, so you can imagine it had seen better days. I didn't care as long as it ran.

After stowing his stuff, Payton hopped into the front seat, excited to finally sit shotgun now the older boys were out of the house.

"Excited for your first day?" I asked.

Payton grunted and stared out the window.

I drove to the middle school, on the other side of town from the high school. I only had to take him to the middle school, and then he walked to hockey practice after school.

"Seventh grade, huh?" I took my hand off the steering wheel long enough to nudge his knee. He didn't react except to move his leg out of my reach.

Five years younger than me, Payton had started each school year by himself where I'd always had Joe, and sometimes Bobby, at my side. My older brothers could be a pain, but they'd been there for me. I tried to do the same for Payton, but the age difference made it difficult. As a result, he'd grown into a bit of a loner.

I pulled up to the curb in front of the middle school. Payton didn't say a word as he picked up his stuff from the back.

"Have a good day, Pay!" I called as the door slammed shut. He didn't acknowledge me, but that wasn't unusual. I hoped he'd keep it together this year. He'd been grounded for most of the summer. We were all hoping with the start of hockey season he'd be too busy to get into trouble.

By the time I pulled into the high school parking lot, most of the spaces had been filled. I drove to the front to the place we'd been parking in since Bobby started driving six years ago, knowing it would be open. Built like a tank and blessed with about as much subtlety, nobody messed with my big brother. Even though he'd graduated three years ago, people still left his spot open for Joe before he graduated and now for me.

Until today.

Today, in Bobby's parking spot, sat a sleek looking Audi.

Thankfully, the driver still sat behind the wheel. Shoving my car into park behind his, I got out, prepared to tell him to get the heck out of my spot.

"Hey! What do you think you're doing? That's my spot," my voice trailed off as the door to the offending car opened and out stepped the most beautiful guy I'd ever seen. With jet black hair and deep olive skin, he had an exotic look that made my heart race.

Swallowing hard, I took in his dark eyes framed by the kind of lashes women paid big bucks for. Usually, I'd think lashes like his were a waste on a guy, but not this one. He deserved every accessory the good Lord blessed him with, if just for my own viewing pleasure.

His perfectly sculpted lips twisted into a scowl, and even that was gorgeous. He could scowl on the front of a teen heartthrob magazine, and they'd fly off the rack.

Then he opened those beautiful lips. "Your spot? Funny, I don't see your name on it." And the words coming out weren't so attractive.

My mouth opened and closed in a decent imitation of a fish before I finally formed a coherent thought. "Yeah, but that doesn't make it any less mine."

His eyes brushed down my body, from my hair to the white tank top I wore with dark wash skinny jeans, bright red Chucks, and one of Joe's old flannel shirts tied around my waist.

I'd never been self-conscious of my appearance before, but this guy's wrinkled brow had me rethinking everything. Which was crazy. I'd been raised to be confident, taught to never change myself to make other people happy. If someone didn't like me for me? Not my problem.

Squaring my shoulders, I recommitted to owning me. Jordan Parks. Tomboy.

"I say it does."

My mouth dropped open. Hypnotic, lyrical voice aside, the words coming out of this dude's mouth grated over my nerves like a loss on the ice. I hated nothing more than losing. Not a game. Not an argument. Not my parking spot.

Fists clenched at my side, I took a step closer to the parking lot interloper. "That. Is. My. Spot."

Dark eyes never leaving mine, he leaned forward, obviously not intimidated by my five-nine frame.

"Not today, it isn't."

For five seconds too long, I let myself get sucked in by his gorgeous good looks. I might have even stared at those perfectly shaped lips. Basically, I lost it just long enough for him to think he had the upper hand.

Unfortunately, he totally did. Without a word, hot guy turned back to his car and opened the back door. He reached inside and removed a guitar case. Then, just before walking away, he glanced over his shoulder and winked.

How dare he!

Buzzing with impotent rage, I marched back to my car with visions of slashing his tires and keying the word 'thief' into his door. But since the school monitored the lot with cameras, I had to satisfy myself with my vivid imagination as I drove to the now only available parking spaces at the back of the lot.

Jerk!

Well, he better believe Jordan Parks wouldn't let him have her spot tomorrow. No, siree. I'd make sure of it. In fact, I hoped he had to lug his stupid guitar from the street.

"What's got you in an uproar this morning?" my friend Natalie asked, falling into step beside me once I'd made it inside.

Hannah and Alex were my camp besties, but Natalie and Kelly were my go-to girls at school.

"Some jerk took my parking spot." Thankful for my tank top, I flapped my elbows at my side to create a breeze. Summer temperatures would soon be a thing of the past, but it wasn't the heat outside making my armpits damp.

Natalie's eyes widened.

"I know, right."

"Probably someone new. No one else would park in that spot. I swear people still think Bobby'll pound 'em if they park there." Natalie shuddered, but she didn't fool me. I knew she had a mild case of hero-worship when it came to my brother. Heck, everyone did. The guy was a freaking legend in these parts. At twenty-one, Bobby lived on the other side of town and went to school at the community college while playing for the minor league hockey team in the next town over. He and Joe shared an apartment, but Joe mostly lived alone during hockey season while Bobby traveled.

"Bobby wouldn't pound anyone," I defended my brother. "At least not off the ice." On the ice was a completely different story, and that's how he earned his reputation. In real life, Bobby was a big ole teddy bear.

"Hey, what's up?" Kelly caught up as we entered the hall where all the senior classes were located. Kelly swam for the swim team and had early morning practice. The scent of chlorine followed her around from September through the end of October. Natalie played volleyball.

Yeah, I rounded out *two* sets of tomboy trios.

"Some douche parked in Jord's spot," Natalie said.

Kelly's eyes widened. "Must be someone new. Who was it?"

"I don't know. I've never seen him before. He had a fancy car, though. And a guitar case." No one carried a guitar case. We had the usual band geeks who lugged around tubas and piccolos, but no guitars. Did school bands even have guitars?

"What did he look like?" Natalie asked.

I knew she'd ask, and I knew my face would turn beet red when she did.

Natalie grinned. "That good, huh? Do you see him now?"

I'd been keeping an eye out. No sign of him. "Nope. And I hope I never see him again."

"It's just a parking spot, Jordan." Leave it to Kelly to be the voice of reason.

"I know. It's just–" That parking spot represented a piece of my brothers, and I missed them. I thought I'd be overjoyed about the boys moving out, but in truth, I hated them being gone. Parking in Bobby's spot made me feel like he was still around looking out for me. And if not him, then Joe. For the last two years, I'd pulled into the parking lot and held onto my identity as Bobby and Joe Parks's little sister. Nobody messed with them, nobody messed with me.

But as Kelly said, it was a parking spot. Anyone had a right to park there. I needed to get over it. It didn't mean I would. And Mr. Parking Spot Thief had just earned himself a spot on my list.

Asher

.　.　.

The sound of a lunch tray clattering down on the table yanked me out of a gripping description of Newton's Laws. Which wouldn't have been so bad except when I glanced up it was her again.

The hot blonde from the parking lot.

And she was not happy.

"Let me guess. This is your table."

What was with this school? Couldn't they make it easy on the new guy and post a sign with all the insider information about assigned parking spaces and lunch tables?

Blondie's eyes narrowed. "What are you doing here?"

I blinked. "Eating?"

She stared daggers.

Two other girls, a brunette and a redhead, flanked her on either side.

The brunette plopped down. "You'll have to excuse her. She's had a bad-" Her eyes widened as she glanced between her friend and me. "Morning."

Blondie shot her friend a look as she took the seat directly across from me.

"You're the one who took Jordan's spot," the redhead said, studying me just a little too carefully. I was used to girls checking me out, but this one looked like she wanted to take a bite out of me.

The dark-haired girl rolled her eyes. "He didn't know it was Jordan's spot, Natalie." She faced me. "You're new, right? I'm Kelly Harris. That's Natalie Chance. And I think you've already met Jordan."

Jordan. A fitting name while everything else seemed such a contradiction. Her clothes tagged her a tomboy, but her face and body were decidedly feminine. The combination worked for her. I liked looking at her more than I wanted to.

"Parks," Jordan added before taking a bite out of an apple.

Parks.

Parks?

Could it be a coincidence? Somehow, I didn't think so.

"Whats's your name?" Natalie asked, still staring a little dreamily.

"Um." I cleared my throat, avoiding her gaze by doing some staring of my own. At Jordan. "Asher. Asher Sloane."

"And you're new?" Kelly asked.

I nodded, and because I didn't want to come across creepy like Natalie, I turned my attention to my food. "Yeah, I just moved from Minnesota."

"Really? How do you like Chicago?"

Lakeview wasn't Chicago, but I noticed everyone lumped the suburb in with the larger city.

I shrugged. "It's nice."

"How come you moved?" Jordan asked, and my heart lurched a little in my chest at the sound of her voice. What was wrong with me?

"Uh, my dad bought a car dealership here."

Three sets of brows rose.

"That explains the fancy car," Jordan murmured under her breath.

For some reason, I felt the need to apologize for what happened earlier, even though I couldn't have possibly known that parking space had been reserved for her.

"I didn't know it was your spot."

"It's fine." She glanced at the uneaten food on her tray. "I think I'm finished." She rose from the table. "See you guys later."

Unable to stop myself, I studied her as she went to dump her tray and set it on the dish return. Her blonde hair hung like a wild mane around her shoulders and down her back. Smooth, tan skin covered her bare shoulders and toned arms. She looked strong, like an athlete. I'd never really been attracted to a girl like her before, but something about Jordan turned my crank.

"What's her story?" I directed my question to Kelly, who seemed more likely to give me a straight answer.

"Who? Jordan? Don't worry about her. She's just been a little stressed lately." The two girls shared a look.

What could be causing Jordan stress?

School? The year just started.

Friends? She didn't seem to have any issues with these two.

Boys? The thought made my jaw clench. Which was dumb. I decided to ask.

"Stressed? How come?" I asked, trying to sound casual. As though I didn't care. And I shouldn't. I didn't even know Jordan. "Boyfriend problems?" Yeah, not casual at all.

Natalie snorted, and Kelly laughed outright.

"Jordan? Boyfriend?" Kelly shook her head. "Funny."

Natalie grinned. "Although her issue does have something to do with boys."

I didn't like the sound of that. "What do you mean?"

"Jordan plays hockey," Natalie said.

My eyes widened. "Hockey? Really?" Even in Minnesota, I hadn't known many girls who played hockey. Jordan's hot points intensified until I thought my attraction to her might incinerate me.

Too bad she probably hated my guts.

"Yes." Kelly nodded.

I frowned. "So, why the stress?"

Natalie and Kelly exchanged glances again, but it was Natalie who spoke up. "Jordan's great at hockey. So good, she made the guys' team. Today is the first practice, and she's a little nervous."

"It doesn't help that her dad's the coach," Kelly added before taking a bite of her lunch.

The girls kept talking, their conversation moving to schoolwork, and their own sports. But I stopped listening, too caught up on the information they'd shared.

Hockey?

All-guys team?

Her dad was the coach?

Parks.

It couldn't be. But the sinking feeling in the pit of my stomach told me it just might.

And if I was right?

I was so screwed.

Blue days, I had Lakeview Singers, an invitation-only choir Ms. Jackson put me in based on my previous choir experience and the fact I played guitar. No way was I the only guy at this school who played, but apparently, I was the only one who played and sang in the choir.

I found a seat on the top tier, glad for a break from my academic classes and anxious to just sing. It didn't take long for the chairs to fill, most of them occupied by girls, but I wasn't the only guy hiding out in the back row.

"Hey, man." A tall guy with long blond hair walked right up to me with his hand extended.

"Hey." I stood up to grip his hand.

"I'm Jarom." He took the seat beside me.

"Asher." I was a little taken aback. Hardly anyone in any of my classes had taken the initiative to introduce themselves to me.

"Man, we gotta stick together in here. These girls," he shook his head, warily scanning the clusters of girls on the tiers below us. "They want to do all this stupid crap. Dancing and-" he shook his head and shuddered a little. "Ms. Jackson's cool, but she goes along with whatever."

This guy was hilarious, I could already tell. "Dude, what are you doing here, then?"

Jarom's eyes met mine. "I'm in a band. We aren't great or anything, but Ms. Jackson's not just a choir director, she's a voice coach. I can't afford lessons, and this is the next best thing." He paused to grin. "Plus, it's a great place to meet hot girls."

I held out my fist, and Jarom tapped it with his.

"Right on, man. So, here's the skinny." He pointed to a cluster of girls front and center. "The one in the middle, in the pink mini skirt? That's Jenna. She thinks she's the best voice in here. Tries to take charge, wants to pick songs. Very annoying. Stay away. Far, far away. In fact..." He paused. I glanced his way again. "Don't date her or any of her friends." He held up his fingers, bent like claws, and hissed.

I was laughing hard at this point. "Got it. What else?"

Jarom pointed again, this time to a quiet girl sitting near Ms. Jackson's piano. She looked sweet and unassuming. "She's the real star. Sasha. Jenna can't stand her because she's by far the best voice in the room. And the nicest girl you'll ever meet, but she's just a sophomore. Let's be real, this class is eighty-five percent women and one-hundred percent drama." Jarom glanced at Sasha again. "I try to keep my eye on that one. She doesn't know how to stand up for herself."

"Right." I could see that. From the top row, Sasha was cute. I had no doubt a girl like Jenna would chew her up and spit her out then grind her into the dirt.

"We have six guys, including you and me. Ms. Jackson likes to do men's choir, so she'll try and have us work on a few songs for concerts." He gave me a look. "We have a lot of concerts."

That was fine with me. I needed all the practice I could get.

Ms. Jackson entered the room, cutting Jarom off. "Okay, everybody, let's get started!" She stood at the front, trying to get everyone's attention. She couldn't be very old, twenties or early thirties at the most. And pretty. I bet there were a few guys who joined choir just because she was kinda hot.

For the first few minutes, she went over the syllabus, concert schedules— Jarom hadn't been kidding; there were a lot— and what to expect over the next few class periods as she determined each of our strengths and weaknesses.

Then, she broke us into groups to get to know each other, so she could call us back individually to sing in one of the practice rooms. Every few minutes, she'd also call out for us to switch groups.

By the time Ms. Jackson called my name, my cheeks were burning from all the female attention as we moved through the groups. Trying to shrug it off, I reminded myself it had more to do with being the new guy than anything else. Pretty soon, they would all forget I was even here.

I snagged my guitar on the way to the practice room. Ms. Jackson sat at a piano, but she spun on the bench when she saw my guitar, her eyes wide and sparkly.

"Is this okay?" I asked, pausing before sitting down.

She nodded. "Absolutely. I'd love to hear you play."

Sitting down across from her, I cleared my throat and wished for a glass of water. I knew I could sing, but I had very little practice singing in front of other people, especially solo. More than anything, I wanted to be a singer/songwriter. So far, it was just a dream, heard mostly by the walls of my bedroom.

I avoided Ms. Jackson's gaze as I strummed the first chord of a song I'd written over the summer. The melody came first, then the words. And for the next three minutes, I sang about dreams and wishes and all the things holding me back, each note, each lyric, a piece of me.

When the song ended, I opened my eyes to find Ms. Jackson watching me. Her mouth hung open, her eyes filled with moisture. She wore the exact expression I dreamed people would have after hearing one of my songs.

"Asher, what was that? I've never heard anything like that before."

"I, um, I wrote it. Did you like it?" I thought I knew the answer, but I kind of wanted to hear her say it.

"Did I like it?" She shook her head a little. "I loved it. That was beautiful."

"Thank you," I said, dipping my head.

"Do you want to sing it? For our fall concert? I always leave spots open for solos or small ensembles. I think you should sing that song." Her eyes widened. "Have you written any others?"

I nodded. "Lots."

"Wow." She stared at me as if she didn't quite know what to do with me. "Wow. Well, you have an amazing talent, Asher. Your voice is beautiful. If your other songs are as good as that one, I can't imagine you won't have an opportunity to do something extraordinary with your music."

"Thank you, Ms. Jackson. I really appreciate that." I stood up. The bell had rung about a minute before.

I made my way to jazz band flying high from Ms. Jackson's praise and the rush of performing, everything about it reaffirming music was my future. No matter what my dad said, I was going to pursue it.

CHAPTER TWO

Jordan

No.

It couldn't be.

Not again.

He turned and spotted me, his lips immediately pulling into a frown before they seemed to change their mind and curve into a smirk.

Another magazine cover pose for him.

What was he doing here?

And how did he make 'jerk' look so good? Not that I cared. I still wanted to be mad at him.

"This your spot, too?" he asked, tipping his head toward his car before reaching into the trunk.

I watched, horrified, as he pulled out a duffle bag and a hockey stick.

"*You* play hockey," I said, the image so incongruous to my preconceived judgments I couldn't even wrap my head around it. After meeting him in the parking lot, I'd almost convinced myself he couldn't possibly be as good-looking as I imagined. But then I saw him in the cafeteria, once again in my spot, and I knew I'd been lying to myself. The boy was hot with a capital *tsss*.

Sizzling.

Asher paused to glare at me. "What's that supposed to mean?"

Since I put my foot in my mouth like a pro regularly, I replied with, "You play the guitar."

And look like a long-lost Jonas brother.

I kept that last part in my head.

"Really? I play the guitar?" He rolled his eyes in a fantastic imitation of a five-year-old as he slammed the trunk shut.

I held my breath as he took a step toward me, lowering his face so close to mine, his breath brushed my cheek. "I'll let you in on a little secret." His voice dipped low into a seductive whisper. "I can do both."

An involuntary shiver raced down my spine.

He turned on his heel and headed into the rink without a backward glance.

Holy smokes!

I'd never experienced that heart-pounding, tingling feeling you read about in romance novels, had begun to wonder if it even existed. It did. I'd experienced it three times that day already.

I held my breath until he disappeared inside the building then gasped, not allowing myself to contemplate what his presence at the rink where my team had practice might mean. I had more important things to worry about, like impressing my dad enough for him to let me start at our first game. I couldn't let myself get distracted by hot guys who stole my parking spot.

And my breath.

Inside the rink, deep male voices echoed off the cinder block walls inside the guy's locker room. As I walked past, a wave of isolation hit me. For the last twelve years, I'd played on an all-girls team. Maybe I'd taken for granted the camaraderie, the sense of being a part of a team that developed inside the locker room.

Not on this team.

At least, not for me. Each day for practice and before every game, I'd prepare alone in a separate locker room.

But I'd made a choice. I wanted to play for the same team as my brothers. The same team coached by my dad. So, I appealed to the commission. They agreed I should be allowed to play as long as I made the team the same as everyone else, by trying out.

And I did. I worked my butt off for a spot on this team.

My thoughts turned to the conversation I had earlier that morning with Hannah and Alex about dating teammates. The stakes were high for me now. I had a lot to prove. The time had come to buckle down, focus. My top priorities had to be hockey and school. I couldn't let anything stand in my way. Especially not a relationship. Which made it doubly important to remember and follow Rule #1. I absolutely could not fall for one of my teammates.

No matter how gorgeous he was.

One good thing about my dad being my coach, I already knew a lot of the players on the team like I knew my own brothers. In fact, one of them was my brother.

Joe skated over as soon as my blades hit the ice. "You ready for this?"

"It's just hockey, Joe. I've been playing since I was five, same as you." I jabbed my stick into the side of his skates, tripping him up and making him laugh. No mercy in the Parks family when it came to our favorite sport.

"You meet the new guy?" I followed his gaze to the place where Asher waited for practice to start, one elbow propped on the wall in front of the bench. He already wore his helmet, making it difficult to see his face even without a face mask.

"At school. He took my parking spot."

Joe snorted. "Want me to beat him up for you?"

"I know. It's silly."

Joe hooked his arm around my neck. "You miss us." I knew Joe would understand. "Wanna move in with Bobby and me?"

I wrinkled my nose and pushed his arm off. "Ew. No. Even if Mom and Dad would let me, it was bad enough when you lived at home and Mom made you guys clean up. I can't even imagine what your apartment looks like, let alone the smell."

Joe cringed. "It is pretty bad. Especially now-"

He didn't have to finish his thought, I knew what he meant. Now he and Chelle, his girlfriend of two years, had broken up, he didn't bother keeping the apartment clean.

"Sorry, Joe-Joe," I reached up to ruffle his hair.

"It's my fault." He batted my hand away from his head. "So, what do you know about the new guy?" He shot me a look. "Other than he took your parking spot."

"Not much. His name's Asher Sloane." And he's hot. Not something I'd admit to my brother. "He's a senior."

From the corner of my eye, I saw my dad stride out onto the ice and put on my helmet. Kevin Parks waited for no man, or woman, if you weren't ready when he said go, you could count on skating until your legs gave out, and then he'd make you skate some more. "He had a guitar."

"Huh. A guitar-playing hockey player. Classy."

Rolling my eyes, I adjusted my chin strap. Honestly, it had nothing to do with whether or not Asher played the guitar, he just didn't fit the profile of a hockey player I had after years of being around a bunch of meatheads. He was just too pretty.

Joe skated in front of me and set his gloved hands on my shoulders. "Seriously, Jord, it's cool you're doing this. I'm excited you're on our team. Don't let these jokers give you a hard time. Play like we taught you. You'll do just fine."

"Thanks, Joe." The sincerity in his eyes threatened to bring tears to mine. Thankfully, he broke up the moment by returning to his usual pain-in-the-butt-self.

"I'm not going to take it easy on you, though, just because you're a girl and my sister. As team captain, it's my job to make sure we play to win. No slacking."

I pushed his shoulder. "When have I ever been a slacker?"

Joe laughed as he skated away from me to center ice where everyone else waited. Everyone except Asher.

And me.

Two outsiders.

Dad blew his whistle. "Line up!"

Asher

I watched Jordan flirt with one of the guys on the team and tried to ignore the stupid pang of jealousy, making my heart feel heavy in my chest. At least, until the guy skated away and I got a good look at his face. Joe Parks. Her brother.

The relief I felt was just as stupid as the jealousy.

I wasn't here to pick up a girlfriend. I wasn't even here to play hockey. I'd shown up to practice for one reason and one reason only, the deal I made with my dad, the one where he let me keep pursuing my music if I kept playing hockey.

Pushing thoughts of my dad to the back of my mind, I focused instead on Jordan. I'd been right. She was hotter than she should have been. Hockey uniforms weren't sexy. At. All. But I knew what it took to play against guys like the ones on this team and the fact she could keep up with them?

Hot.

I couldn't keep my eyes off her. Which was how I ended up beside her on the goal line when Coach began calling out drills.

"Stalking me, Sloane?" she asked.

"I showed up first every time today. Maybe you're stalking me." Coach blew his whistle. We both took off. Jordan had to be at least six inches shorter than me, but she was fast. We reached the goal line within nanoseconds of each other, slid into a hockey stop, turning quickly to go back.

Once we'd all returned to the start, Coach blew his whistle again. We skated backward.

"Why would I want to do that?" she asked, keeping her voice low.

Why indeed? I knew a lot of girls found me attractive. I didn't miss the way Jordan's eyes widened when I got out of my car this morning. I liked the idea of her being attracted to me.

"You tell me," I said, giving her my best smolder.

Her mouth dropped open before she could catch herself. She schooled her features into a bored mask. "Does that usually work for you?"

I winked. "All the time, gorgeous." I hadn't meant to add that last part, it just slipped out.

She made a disgusted sound, making me laugh.

"Something funny, Sloane?" Coach yelled over the noise of everyone's skates.

"No, sir!"

Crap.

As my coach and Jordan's dad, I did not want to be on Coach Parks's bad side. Putting my head down, I focused on skating. After a few seconds, I glanced over at Jordan. She caught me. I widened my eyes with a grin. Instead of smiling back, she scowled, and for some reason, I cared.

Coach blew his whistle again. And again. Back and forth, we completed warmups, skating forward, backward, forward again but jumping the lines, then with the puck. Jordan skated as though she had something to prove. With her shorter legs, she had to work harder to keep pace with me. I wondered if she'd done any speed training. My dad could be a bit of a fanatic. He sent me to every kind of training for speed, strength, agility. He even made me do yoga.

Little did he know I had no intention of pursuing hockey after high school. His dreams of me playing at the next level were just that, dreams. I'd play by his rules until I graduated, but then I had every intention of following in my mother's footsteps straight to the microphone. All without worrying about my dad and what he wanted.

I didn't hate hockey. I'd been playing long as I could remember. The hockey stick felt like an extension of my arm. Like a basketball player dribbling the ball, handling the puck required skill, practice. And like basketball players, some had better skills than others.

Jordan knew what she was doing.

"You're good," I murmured just loud enough for her to hear as we crossed the line.

She shot me a dirty look. "For a girl, you mean."

I shook my head. "I'd never say that."

Girl or not, daughter or not, she had to be good to play for Kevin Parks. He didn't have the winningest record in the state for nothing.

We were teammates. I hated that we'd gotten off on the wrong foot. That meant we needed a truce.

"Hey, I'm sorry about earlier. I didn't know that was your spot. And at lunch, too. Can't you cut the new guy some slack?" We'd just finished the last of the skating drills. Around us, everyone breathed hard. If you didn't sweat off five pounds at hockey practice, you weren't doing it right.

Jordan bent slightly at her waist, sucking air. She lifted her head, settling her gaze on me. Her eyes slid from the top of my head, over my face, down my neck and shoulders until they stopped.

Her eyes flew to mine.

"You're left-handed."

I glanced at the offending hand before meeting her blue-eyed gaze again. "Yeah. So?"

"I'm left-handed."

I'd noticed but still didn't see what she was getting at.

"Don't you get it?" She clenched her jaw, shaking her head just a little. "How many left-handed players do you think there are on this team, genius?"

Frowning, I wondered where she was going with this. "Not many."

"That's right. Not many. Only three, including you and me."

She slung the words like mud, and they hit me, splattered across my face. There were two left-handed positions on the ice at a time.

We might be teammates, but every week, Jordan and I would compete for the same spot. And from the look on her face, if I hadn't already earned the title, I'd just become public enemy number one.

CHAPTER THREE

Jordan

Usually, I didn't wait for my dad after practice. I had a car of my own, and he had things he needed to do before he could leave. I waited just outside his office door until he glanced up from his computer.

"Hey, pretty girl," he rose from his desk and walked around it with his arms outstretched.

"You probably don't want to hug me, Dad."

He wrapped me in a familiar hug. "I'm not scared."

I held him tight, basking in the security of his embrace. I needed it after today.

"What's the matter, kiddo?" he asked, planting a kiss on the top of my head before pulling back to search my eyes.

I shrugged, wishing I knew the answer myself.

Dad frowned, placing his hands on my shoulders. "You worried about something? Did something happen at school today?"

I shook my head.

"You're worried about the team?" His expression hardened. "Did anyone give you a hard time today? The new guy? I saw the two of you talking."

"No, Dad. Nothing like that." Asher kind of was the problem, but not in the way my dad thought.

"Then what?"

I bit my lip, glancing down. But Dad wasn't having it, chucking my chin until my eyes met his.

I shrugged again. "I just—" How could I explain how I felt, how much I wanted this? Playing hockey had been my dream all my life. I knew he understood, but— "Asher. He's left-handed." He already knew, of course.

"Ahhh." Dad's eyes narrowed. He took a step back and crossed his arms over his chest, visibly changing roles from 'Dad' to 'coach'. For a long moment, he studied me with an expression I recognized. He wouldn't tell me what I wanted to hear, he'd tell the truth whether I was ready or not.

"I told you when you asked me to help you talk to the commission, I couldn't give you any special favors, Jordan. You'd have to earn your spot on my team, the same as everybody else. I decide before every game who will put us in the best position to win, and they start in games. But that doesn't mean anyone will ride the bench all season. You know as well as I do this is a demanding sport. I need my bench to be just as strong as my starting lineup."

I nodded because I did know. "But, Dad—" I swallowed hard against the emotions clogging my throat. "Dad, if I don't start, what are my real chances of getting noticed by anyone? I want to play at the next level. I don't want to be done when I'm too old to play in the junior league."

Dad reached a hand up to the back of his neck and sighed. "I know, sweetheart, and I think you made the best decision to get you there by coming to play for me. But, Jordan, I have nineteen guys on this team who deserve the same shot you have. Asher included. I can't show you any special treatment even if I want to do just that. But what I can do is give you the best training and coaching I know."

"I know. I just—" I sniffed, rubbing the back of my hand under my nose.

Colleges didn't look at second-string. They wanted the best. And the best started. Justin Painter, the only other left-handed player on our team, was a bruiser, perfect for left-side defense, leaving left-wing to me. Until Asher showed up. Now it would be a competition every week for the starting position. Dad would never put me in a defensive position, I didn't have the build. But I had what it took as a winger, fast, tough, smart. I knew the game of hockey inside and out. You didn't have to be left-handed to play on the left side, but it provided a clear advantage, one I'd planned to exploit.

But now?

Now, I'd have to work doubly hard to earn my spot. I didn't fear hard work, I'd put in the time, but would it be enough?

Dad took a deep breath. "Look, I know what you're thinking, but you can't worry about Asher or anyone else. All you can do is play *your* game, do *your* best, and I'll be frank, honey, if your best doesn't cut it to start on my team, then you aren't ready for what's out there."

That hurt and did little to calm my anxiety.

"Jordan, look at me." He waited until I did. "You have the one thing I can't teach these other guys, and that's heart. You want this, so go get it. Work harder than anyone, listen to what I teach you, and the rest will take care of itself. Okay?"

I nodded. He hugged me again as I inhaled his comforting scent. I'd always been a daddy's girl. I used to love sitting on his lap as a little girl while he watched hockey on the television. My love of the game intertwined with my love for my dad.

"Thanks, Daddy."

He squeezed the breath from me, making me laugh.

"I'll see you at home," he said, releasing me to sit behind his desk again while I headed toward the door. "Hey, Jord?"

I turned to face him. "Yeah?"

"I love you, kiddo. As important as this is to you and as much as you want it, hockey isn't everything. Don't forget to live your life while you pursue your dreams."

"I love you, too. And I'll try."

. . .

Dinner used to be my favorite time of day when everyone finally got home, and we sat around the table talking and joking. I've always loved the sense of security when we were all together. I didn't like change under most circumstances, but especially when it came to my family. First, Bobby moved out, then Joe. Now they only came around on Sunday afternoons for Mom's pot roast and to use the washer and dryer. I'd see Joe every day at hockey practice, but it wasn't the same as it used to be when we were younger. With only the four of us at the table, the silence just felt awkward.

"How was the first day of school?" Mom asked, her eyes flicking between Payton and me.

The scowl on my younger brother's face answered well enough. Mom looked at me.

"Oh, um," I stammered. "It was fine. Good."

Mom set her fork down on her plate. "Fine? Good? That's all I get? How were your classes? Did you see Natalie and Kelly?"

Okay, we were sharing. I liked it better when the older boys were around to make a joke of everything.

"Classes were fine. I have some homework. Natalie and Kelly were there. I don't have any classes with them, which kind of stinks."

Mom picked up her fork again. "Well, that's okay. You'll have an opportunity to meet new people."

"Not many new kids when you've been going to the same school since kindergarten, Mom." Except for Asher, whom I'd run into more times than I wanted.

"We have a new guy on the team," Dad spoke to Mom but winked at me. "His name's Asher."

I narrowed my eyes. What was he up to?

"He's new at school, too, isn't he?" Dad held back a chuckle.

I rolled my eyes. Dad got a kick out of teasing me.

"A new boy at school?" Mom asked, overly interested. "What's he like?"

I shrugged. "I don't know. I didn't talk to him much."

I kicked Payton under the table. He looked up, ready for a fight. I widened my eyes at him, praying he'd understand my silent communication to join the conversation and save me.

"What about you, Pay? How was your day?" I asked when he remained quiet.

"And he plays hockey?" Mom asked as though I hadn't even spoken to Payton.

I shot my brother a dirty look, but he just grinned. "Yeah, he plays hockey. And he's a senior. That's about all I know about him." That and he wanted to steal my starting position.

Darn Asher Sloane!

"Did you know his family moved into the Cunningham's house behind us?"

My fork clattered to my plate. "No way."

Dad nodded, continuing to eat as though he hadn't just dropped a bomb on my dinner. "I didn't make the connection until last night when I went over everyone's registration paperwork and noticed the address."

Awesome.

My teammate/enemy was also my neighbor.

For the next two hours, I avoided my favorite place, my bedroom. Being the only girl had its benefits, the best, having my own room. It served as a haven away from my brothers when they got on my nerves, a place to secretly stalk Shawn Mendes on Instagram without getting teased. In short, I loved my bedroom.

And suddenly, because of one Asher Sloane, I also feared it.

Why?

Because it faced the Cunningham's old house.

Asher might have been on my last nerve, but I couldn't deny the guy intrigued me. He had his good looks. He played hockey. And who didn't like a guy who played guitar?

Which was why I didn't want to go into my room. I knew if I did, I'd be tempted to stand at my window to try and catch a glimpse of the new family who practically shared our backyard.

Who was I kidding?

I didn't want to see his family.

I wanted to see Asher.

So, I stayed downstairs and worked on my homework at the table. Then, I took my time in the shower, shaving my legs and giving my hair a good wash until the steam filling the bathroom grew so thick I could barely see.

With my shower finished, I couldn't put it off any longer. I had to go into my room or spend the rest of the night in a bath towel. After slipping through the door like a thief in the night, I tiptoed over to the window. I left the light off and made sure to stand to the side because getting caught half-naked by my new neighbor would just be the perfect ending to a perfectly crappy day.

I loved the evening when the sun set, and the oranges and reds softened to pinks and violets. My bedroom still felt warm from the afternoon sun. I wrapped my towel more securely around my body and with one hand, while standing to the side, opened the window just enough to allow a slight breeze into my room. Only the breeze didn't come alone, it brought something with it.

Mesmerized, I dropped to the carpet below my window.

At first, I only heard the guitar. Then, as my ears adjusted, Asher. It had to be him. I didn't recognize the melody or the lyrics, but his voice. Even after such a short time, I knew his voice.

The music stopped. I waited. He began again, repeating what he'd just sung only to cut himself off once more. For the next thirty minutes, I sat under my window in my dark room wearing nothing but a damp bath towel, straining my ears to hear every note, every lyric.

I could listen to him forever.

"Asher!" a man's voice called. My heart raced as though I'd been caught eavesdropping.

"Yeah!" Asher called back, his voice clear and a lot closer than I expected.

I rolled to my knees and peeked enough to see Asher's long strides carry him across the yard to the back door of his house. The dark silhouette of a man filled the opening. He stepped aside, allowing Asher to cross the threshold before closing the door.

Glancing down, I realized I still wore my towel. I hadn't even gotten dressed. I'd been so engrossed listening to Asher.

Asher.

The boy who threatened my chance at achieving my goals.

I needed to get a grip.

It didn't matter what he looked like. Or if he had the most amazing voice. Because my new neighbor had become my number one enemy.

Asher

"How was hockey practice?" Dad called me in from the backyard, where I'd been working on a new song before dinner.

My step-mom, Shari, wanted us to eat dinner together as a family. I didn't mind, except it usually turned into an inquisition.

Typical. My first day at a new school, my senior year no less, and all he cared about was hockey. I had to leave my friends behind and start a new school so close to graduation because of him. You'd think he'd be a little sympathetic. But no. Not my dad.

"Fine," I replied. I pushed a pile of peas around my plate, hoping it would make them disappear. If I could get away with it, I'd slip them onto my baby brother's high chair tray. At ten months old, Caleb would eat just about anything you put in front of him. It didn't even have to be food.

"And how about school?" Shari asked, forcing a cheerful smile. "How was your first day?"

I liked Shari. She had a way of softening the rough edges my dad developed after my mom left us when I was two years old. Shari and I weren't necessarily close, but I figured we needed her. It had been an adjustment when Dad married her five years ago and even more so when Caleb came along. But Dad seemed happy.

"First day was good." If it had just been Shari, I might have told her about the incident in the parking lot with Jordan. She would get a kick out of it. Dad would ask too many questions, which would lead to him realizing Jordan was Coach Parks's daughter. He'd tell me not to aggravate her to stay on Coach's good side.

Everything revolved around hockey with him.

"You're lucky to have a spot on Kevin Parks's team, Asher. Don't take it for granted. This is an incredible opportunity for you. You're a talented athlete."

Clenching my jaw against the disrespectful words aching to get out, I stared at my nearly full plate. We'd had this discussion before. Dad wanted me to play hockey. I wanted to pursue my music. He hated everything about my love of music and refused to acknowledge any amount of talent I might possess.

Like I said before, I didn't blame him. But just because she chose music over us didn't mean I would turn out like her and do what she did. She hurt me, too. I'd never make the same mistakes as her. Sure, I'd make my own, but that was life. Right?

Hockey wasn't my passion.

Dad had to stop playing competitive hockey as a sophomore in college because his leg got crushed in a car accident. He could walk, but he couldn't skate, not enough to play hockey.

Somehow his dream for himself had become his dream for me. It sure wasn't the dream I had for myself. Not even close. I knew Dad wished I'd inherited his love for hockey rather than Mom's love of music, but I didn't.

"Don't worry, Dad. I haven't forgotten our agreement. May I be excused?"

Dad frowned but nodded.

I put my dish in the sink and went up to my room.

What a day.

I flopped on my back on my bed and let my thoughts turn Jordan. I hadn't been able to get her off my mind.

I knew from what her friends had said at lunch, she'd likely show up at the same hockey practice as me, but it had still been a shock when she arrived in the parking lot outside the rink.

I hardly knew what to do with the wave of attraction I felt. Despite being a raving lunatic that morning, everything about her hit me in all the right ways. If she hadn't been screaming at me, I might have asked to walk in with her.

Seeing her at lunch had only reinforced the physical attraction. I liked the way she dressed. Kind of edgy. A lot sexy. It was apparent she had no idea, which just added to her appeal. And her hair. So soft and feminine.

During practice, I'd had to skate my butt off to keep up with her. I admired her determination, her drive. She was fierce. The girl could play. Everything about her effort on the ice testified her love of the game.

Even the fear in her eyes when she realized we'd be competing for the same position on the ice told me Jordan's passion for the sport far exceeded my own.

I wanted to reassure her I didn't care about hockey, and she could have the starting position without any kind of competition from me, but that wouldn't fly. My dad expected me to do my best, which meant working my tail off to start in games. Either that or I knew he'd make good on his threat to my dreams.

And I just couldn't let that happen.

The next day at school, I gave in to the temptation to yank Jordan's chain and showed up to school early to park in her spot again. I shouldn't have done it. It made me a douche for sure, but I wanted to talk to her. We were teammates. And even though we'd be competing for the starting position, we still had to play as a team.

I leaned back against the trunk and waited.

About five minutes later, Jordan came barreling into the parking lot. By the expression on her face, I'd done the exact wrong thing if I wanted to make amends. I just hoped she'd forgive me since I'd scared off two different people who tried to park in the spot next to me, so she didn't have to go all the way to the back.

She parked jaw set and avoided my gaze as she got out of her car.

"Jordan! Wait!" I called, chasing after her. She didn't even hesitate, just kept going. Well, what did I expect?

I couldn't move very fast with my guitar case banging against my legs, but I still caught up. Walking backward in front of her, I got an eyeful of just how angry I'd made her.

"Jordan, I'm sorry. I was just messing around."

She moved to side-step around me, but I got in her way again.

"Come on. If I really meant to be a jerk, I wouldn't have saved you a spot next to me." I gave her my most charming smile.

Stopping short, she planted her fist on one hip. "If you didn't want to be a jerk, you should have parked in the other spot and let me have mine."

She was right, of course. "But that wouldn't have been as funny."

Her lips flattened into a thin line.

I put up my hands between us, signaling my surrender. "Fine. I'm sorry. It was just a joke. I do want to talk to you, though."

She started walking again. "Too bad. I don't want to talk to you."

Before she could go too far, I caught hold of her wrist. She stopped with a gasp, her eyes wide and mouth open.

Maybe I'd been the one to go too far.

I dropped her wrist. "Sorry." I ran my fingers through my hair, irritated with this whole situation. "Listen, I don't know what the big deal is about your parking spot, but I won't park there again. I just wanted to talk to you and was trying to be funny." I made a face. "Epic fail. Message received. But come on, we're on the same team. I don't want to fight with you."

She didn't say anything, just stared at me so long my ears get hot. Finally, she lifted her chin and took a step toward me, the top of her head barely reaching my chin.

"Teammate or not, hockey is my life," she said, poking my chest with her finger. "Don't mess with me or my game. Got it? We are not friends."

Good hell, she was gorgeous.

Heart in my throat, it was all I could do to nod.

"Good." She jabbed me again for good measure before spinning on her heel and walking away.

Convinced she was wrong, I waited until she disappeared to start down the hall in the opposite direction to put away my guitar. We were teammates, and if I had anything to say about it, we wouldn't just be friends, we'd be more.

CHAPTER FOUR

Jordan

I'd only met Asher Sloane twenty-four hours ago, and already he drove me crazy! Just who did he think he was, anyway? Parking in my spot. Trying to take my place on the team. Well, he could just go right back where he came from!

"Wow. Two mornings in a row?" Natalie asked, eyes wary.

"Ugh! It's that Asher guy. He's determined to ruin my senior year."

Natalie frowned. "What, did he park in your spot again?"

"Yes, but you were right. It's a stupid parking spot. It's that he did it just to make me mad." He said he did it to be funny, but I didn't believe him. The guy was out to get me.

"Why would he want to do that?"

I shrugged. "Because he's a jerk? And I hate him?"

Natalie made a face. "You don't even know him. How can you hate him?"

"Stop being so reasonable!"

"Who's being reasonable?" Kelly asked, joining us with wet hair and a fresh face.

Natalie rolled her eyes. "I think the real question is who's being *un*reasonable."

"You're supposed to be on my team, Nat."

Natalie threw up her arms. "I am. I'm just saying, give the guy a chance. He's only been here one day."

"Really? This again? What did he do this time?" Kelly shook her head, clearly exasperated.

"He parked in her spot again." Natalie pumped her eyebrows at Kelly.

Kelly's lips split into a grin. "Did he, now?"

"What's that supposed to mean," I asked.

Kelly flipped her hair over her shoulder. "It means he's a delicious piece of eye candy, and he's flirting with you."

My jaw dropped. "No, he isn't! How could you say that?"

Kelly glanced at Natalie. "She's in denial."

Natalie nodded, agreeing wholeheartedly.

"I am not! And it doesn't matter anyway. He's my *teammate*." I took a second to relish the satisfaction of shutting them both up. "And you know the rule, no falling for a teammate."

"But you've thought about it," Natalie said. "You've thought about it or you wouldn't have brought up the rule. Admit it. You think he's GOR-geous."

I inhaled a deep breath filled with long-suffering and reminded myself I'd been friends with these two for a decade, too long to turn my back on them for being such complete ninnies!

"It doesn't matter if I think he's good-looking." And heaven only knew, I did! "He's my teammate and a parking spot thief."

Not to mention, he had a beautiful singing voice and had it out for my starting position on the hockey team. But I couldn't reveal my secret, that I'd become an eavesdropper and a self-doubter. That kind of negativity didn't deserve a voice.

"And he's hawt!" Natalie sighed.

I threw up my hands. "I'm outta here. You two are hopeless. See you at lunch." I walked away to the sounds of their snickers. Traitors!

We'd just see about them and their theories. Asher Sloane would never be interested in a tomboy like me, although the thought did send a thrill of excitement through me so strong I shuddered. Parking in my spot for the second day in a row had to be his idea of mind games. That's all there was to it.

Determined not to let Asher get to me, I pushed all thoughts of him to the back of my mind and tried to focus on school. Getting onto a college team wouldn't be easy, even more so if I didn't keep up with my grades.

By lunch, I needed a break. Anxiety about running into Asher again threatened to choke me. Thankfully, Natalie and Kelly sat alone at our usual table. I heaved a sigh of relief. But where was Asher? I found him sitting with Jarom and a couple of his friends. They were in a band. It made sense Asher would make friends with them.

"I see Asher didn't want to take his life in his own hands by crashing our table again today," Kelly teased.

I set my tray down and scowled. "Can we please have a conversation that doesn't revolve around Asher?" He'd been consuming my thoughts since the day before. I didn't want to talk about him anymore.

Kelly shrugged. "Sure, what do you want to talk about?"

"Ooh, I know! Why don't we talk about the transfer student from Lakes High?" Natalie grinned.

Kelly whirled on Natalie. "How did you hear about him?"

"How did I not hear about him? Who is he?" I asked.

"He's not quite as good-looking as your boy, Asher, but whew!" Natalie fanned herself with her hand. "He is fi-ine."

Kelly rolled her eyes. "Yeah, if you're into arrogant jocks."

"What's this arrogant jock's name?" I asked Natalie because Kelly's poopy face put me off.

"Jared Oliver."

Wait. "Haven't I heard that name before?"

Natalie nodded excitedly, but Kelly's expression gave me the real answer.

"Wasn't he the guy-" I started to say.

"Yes," Kelly cut me off. "Let's talk about something else. How about this, Natalie kissed Finn over the summer and didn't tell anyone."

Natalie gasped, her face turning bright red. "How do you know about that?"

"Wait. You did kiss Finn over the summer? Nat, what the heck? How could you not tell us?" Someone scrape me off the floor! This was big news. Big.

"No one was supposed to know." Natalie looked close to tears. "How did you find out?" she asked Kelly.

Kelly crossed her arms over her chest. "Why are you keeping secrets, Nat? We're best friends."

Natalie jumped to her feet. "Are we, though?" she cried, a single tear rolling down her cheek. "Because best friends don't blab things they know nothing about!" Without another word, she stormed from the cafeteria, leaving her lunch tray and Kelly and me both gaping after her.

"What in the world just happened?"

Kelly's shoulders drooped. "I shouldn't have brought it up like that. It's my fault."

She wasn't wrong. She shouldn't have, but I had a feeling I understood why she did. Natalie liked to tease us about boys. There had to be something I didn't understand going on with Kelly and this Jared dude that Natalie knew about.

"Did she kiss Finn? For real?" I asked, my voice barely above a whisper. Finn was Natalie's older brother, Charlie's best friend. She'd had a crush on him since third grade, but Finn and Charlie graduated with Joe, so they were older than us.

Kelly nodded. "Yeah, I heard about it from Angie. They were all at a party this summer. I don't know the details. Angie didn't, either. I just know it happened." Angie was Kelly's older sister, even older than Finn and Charlie, but they all went to school together in Champaign at the University of Illinois.

"And the transfer student?" I asked.

Kelly shook her head and rose from her seat. "I'll see you later."

What the heck was going on around here?

Asher

.   .   .

Thank goodness for Jarom. Because of him, I didn't have to be the loser with no one to sit with during lunch. He introduced me to the other two guys in his band, Bash and Adam, and then proceeded to give me the who's who of the senior class in his unique and hilarious way.

"Who you starin' at, bro?" he asked out of the blue.

"What do you mean?" I replied startled. Of course, I'd been watching Jordan, not at all realizing I'd been so obvious about it. I felt terrible for the way things went down earlier and wondered exactly what I could do to fix it. Other than parking as far away from 'her' spot as possible.

Jarom sat back in his chair with a smirk. "I knew you had your eyes on someone."

"Who?" Jarom's friend, Adam, spoke up. Adam was kind of quiet and looked exactly like you would think a guy in a high school garage band would. He played the guitar and wore dark skinny jeans, a black shirt, and a leather jacket. His dark hair hung low over his brow, making it so he constantly reached up to brush it out of his eyes.

"Nobody." No way I'd admit anything to these clowns.

Jarom squinted at the table where Jordan sat with her two friends. They seemed to be having an intense discussion making me kind of wish we were close enough to eavesdrop.

"Jordan?" he guessed.

I snorted. "Jordan? Yeah, right. She's on my hockey team."

Jarom's brows pulled low. He leaned onto the back two legs of his chair to peer around the table beside us to get a look at Jordan where she sat with Kelly and Natalie across the room.

"Seriously?" he asked.

I kicked his chair, almost making him lose his balance. "Dude! What are you doing? Stop staring."

Jarom sat forward and grinned. "You do like her."

I shook my head, ready to deny it to the death.

"Good luck with that," Adam said.

"Yeah, man," Bash agreed. Bash played the drums, and where Adam was all things dark, Bash looked like he just stepped off the plane from California. Bleach blond hair, blue eyes, white shorts, and a baby blue shirt. Since he sat down, he'd been tapping out rhythms non-stop using pencils, utensils, even his fingers.

"What do you mean? Not that he's right." I jabbed my thumb at Jarom, who just smiled.

Bash sat forward, leaning his elbows on the table. "Jordan Parks may be smokin', but I've never seen her with a single guy at this school. Not once."

"I don't think she's ever had a boyfriend," Adam added.

Jarom glanced Jordan's way again. "It's a real tragedy."

I didn't know how I felt about these guys talking about Jordan being hot, but it wasn't good. "Why not?" I hesitated to ask, but only for about a split second. These guys had information and I wanted it.

Jarom shrugged. "I'm not sure. But I think it might have something to do with the fact she's hella intimidating. Have you seen that girl? Her biceps are bigger than mine."

I glanced at Jarom's arms and figured it didn't take much.

He followed the direction of my gaze and frowned. "Not cool, man."

I grinned, already knowing him well enough to know I hadn't offended him.

"Not only is she intimidating, so are her brothers. Bobby Parks is a freaking legend at this school. Nobody messes with him or his." Adam shuddered.

Of course, I knew about Jordan's brothers. Bobby was twenty-one and played in the minors. Joe was nineteen and played on the same team as Jordan and me. Joe seemed cool, but then, I'd never given him a reason to hate me.

Yeah, I guess I understood what they were getting at.

"Okay, so dudes are too chicken to ask her out, but hasn't she ever liked anyone?" It kind of slew me she'd never dated anyone. A girl like Jordan should have guys hanging all around her. Not that it hurt my feelings she didn't.

All three guys shook their heads.

"Not that I've ever heard," Bash said.

Jarom narrowed his gaze at me. "What about you, man? If you don't have a thing for Jordan, then what? You got a girl back where you came from?"

We hadn't discussed my move.

I shook my head. "Nope. No girlfriend." At least, not anymore. "Not interested in the long-distance thing."

All this talk about Jordan and girlfriends had my fingers itching to play my guitar.

"Listen, I'm gonna go play my guitar. I'll catch you guys later." Reaching for my bag, I got ready to leave.

Adam snorted. "You sound as bad as me. Maybe you should join our band."

I rolled my eyes, not taking him seriously. "Right."

But Jarom sat up straight, his mouth dropped open. "That's a great idea. You should totally join our band."

I sat back, glancing at Adam and Bash to gauge their reaction. They didn't seem at all wigged out by Jarom speaking up for the three of them.

"You guys barely know me." I'd never been part of a band. I'd always imagined a solo career. Like my mom. "You don't even know if I can sing."

"Yes, I do, man. I heard you singing yesterday. The door to the practice room wasn't closed all the way. You can sing." Jarom watched me with hopeful eyes.

Adam made a face. "He's been talking about it ever since."

"Look, I can sing, but even just hearing you sing one song, I can tell you're better." Jarom wanted this, I could tell.

"So, how would it work?" I couldn't believe I was considering it. I had no idea when I'd have time to practice or how I would explain it to my dad, but I wanted it.

Jarom nodded, the start of a smile curling his lips. "Right on, man." He sat forward, bracing his elbows on the table. "We can work things out, but you'd be our lead, Bash on drums, Adam, guitar. I play the piano, but don't tell Ms. Jackson."

Pulling my chin back, I stared at him. "You play the piano?"

"Dude, shh. Seriously, don't tell anyone. Ms. Jackson will make me accompany the choir if you do." He glanced around dramatically. "With you and Adam on guitar and us singing." He shrugged and kind of let the implication hang there.

"My dad's not super supportive of my music."

The three of them exchanged glances.

"Yeah, we get that. None of our parents are either."

"And I have hockey." I'd quit hockey today and spend every day practicing with these guys, even if they were terrible. My dad would have a fit and disown me.

Jarom nodded. "Maybe we can work something out with Ms. Jackson during advising or something. I'm not sure. But we'll do what it takes to make it happen. We don't have any gigs right now, but I think if we work, we can audition for some local shows."

Wow. Jarom had bigger dreams than I expected. I kind of thought they just messed around for fun, but from the expressions on all their faces, I'd underestimated them.

"Yeah. Okay. I'm in." And I'd deal with my dad when the time came, which would hopefully be way, way in the future.

All three guys sagged with apparent relief.

"Awesome." Jarom stood, his fist extended.

And just like that, I'd joined a band.

CHAPTER FIVE

Jordan

I didn't see much of Asher the rest of the first week of school, and everything seemed to be falling into place as it should. No one parked in my parking spot. Asher sat with Jarom and his friends at lunch. Natalie and Kelly apologized and made up after squabbling at lunch. And after practice that first day, we seemed to form some unspoken agreement to skate on opposite ends of the rink for drills. During scrimmage, since we played the same position, we never scrimmaged on the same team and we never had to go against each other.

Instead, I battled Leo Jessup.

Play to win.

"Oomph." My shoulder hit the wall. Leo's huge body pinned me for a split second before he backed off, grinning.

Too bad Leo wanted to maim me before we could even play our first game.

"Idiot! We're on the same team." I'd been going home with sore shoulders from all the body checks into the wall. Leo outweighed me by at least fifty pounds and seemed to get a kick out of smashing me.

The first couple of days, I thought he just played a physical game, or maybe he wanted to make a point to the new girl, but now, I kind of thought it might be his own unique brand of flirting.

Gross.

"Dude, what is your problem?" From out of nowhere, Asher skated full speed at Leo. They crashed into the wall. "You trying to get her injured before our first game?"

Leo untangled himself from Asher with a smirk. "Got a thing for her, man?" he said, skating backward and making an obscene gesture.

Asher didn't even glance my way before skating after him to join the game again.

It started and ended so fast, no one else even noticed. Guys pushed each other around all the time. However, for the rest of practice, Asher made it his business to hit Leo any chance he got. By the end, other guys began to notice and run interference. I half expected Dad to step in, but he let them play. You had to be tough to play hockey. Fighting came with the territory.

However, I didn't need some new kid fighting my battles.

I went and changed like always, but instead of getting into my car, I waited beside his.

Guys trickled out of the building. If any of them noticed me standing there, none of them said anything. I only hoped Joe would be the last guy out like usual. This conversation didn't require any brotherly interference.

I figured half the team had gone home before Asher came walking out. My heart beat faster at the sight of him, which only made me angry. I didn't want to be attracted to him.

Asher caught sight of me, his eyes lighting at first, but then his brows pulled low. "What did I do now?" he asked.

"I have three brothers. I don't need another one."

"You think that was me being brotherly?"

The way he said it made my cheeks flush. "It doesn't matter. I don't need you or anyone else protecting me. I can take care of myself."

Asher shook his head as he stepped around me to open the trunk of his car. He tossed his gear in the back with more force than necessary and slammed the trunk shut.

I stood in front of the driver's side door. Asher strode toward me, his jaw clenched. How did he manage to be so pretty and masculine all at the same time?

"That guy was out of line." Asher braced a hand on the roof of his car and leaned close.

"My problem. Not yours." He smelled good after his shower. Having three brothers, I'd become more familiar with masculine scents than I wanted, but Asher used something I'd never noticed before. I liked it.

"You're my teammate," he countered.

"So is Leo."

Asher frowned. "He's not acting like it."

He might be right, but that didn't change anything. "I don't. Need. Your. Help." I punctuated each word with a jab to his chest with my finger.

His frown deepened. "Fine."

"Fine."

"Good."

It occurred to me how close we were. My hand still touched his chest. I brought it back as though he'd burned me.

I nodded. "Good. I'm glad we cleared that up."

His lips twisted with the beginnings of a smile. "Me, too. Now, are you going to let me in my car or not?" He gestured to his door, the one I still blocked.

Mustering as much dignity as I was capable of, I walked to my car. It wasn't until I started the ignition I noticed Asher hadn't moved to get into his car. Instead, he stood there, still watching me. I probably should have felt creeped out, but I didn't. His eyes followed me out of the parking lot. I gasped at the wave of emotion passing over me from the heat of his stare.

I didn't want to like Asher, but no way could I deny my attraction.

"It doesn't matter," I admonished myself out loud. We were teammates. And enemies. I couldn't have a crush on Asher Sloane.

No crush didn't mean I couldn't love his music. Over the next couple of weeks, it became my ritual to shower after dinner and sit under my open window in shorts and a sports bra while icing my shoulder while listening to Asher sing and play his guitar. He went outside every night. And after just a few weeks, I already dreaded the colder weather that would soon keep him from unwittingly serenading me.

We still had another couple of weeks before our first game. Practices became more intense, and so did the pressure to play well. Leo let up a little on the ice after Asher laid into him, but the look in his eye said we weren't finished.

Things weren't only tense on the ice, they were rocky at home, too.

"Jordan, take your plate up to your room," Dad said one night as I went to sit down in my usual chair at the dinner table.

"O-kay," I murmured, backing away from the table. I hadn't noticed earlier, but the air in the dining room felt thick with tension. My little brother sat with his head down, his hands in his lap. Dad's jaw twitched. He fisted a napkin in his hand. Mom's worried gaze flicked back and forth between father and son.

Tempting as it might be to sit at the top of the stairs and listen to the drama unfold at the dinner table, I didn't. Whatever was going on with Payton, I wished he'd figure it out. I hated seeing him get in trouble. And I didn't know how much more my parents could take.

I closed my bedroom door to block out the raised voices downstairs. I looked to my window but doubted Asher would be outside this early. I didn't think he'd realized we lived so close to each other yet. He hadn't caught me listening to him, but that could be because I didn't sit there and stare at him through the window. I made sure to remain out of sight, content to hear him even if I couldn't see him.

Which said something about his singing, because not looking was a sacrifice. I'd never considered myself boy crazy before, but the boy next door had quickly become an obsession.

I even found myself watching for him in the halls between classes, before and after school in the parking lot, and I'd cast enough glances his way during lunch to have drawn the attention of my two best friends.

Not that it mattered. I would never date Asher Sloane. Even if he wasn't entirely out of my league as far as looks went, we were teammates. I needed to think of him as the enemy. I'd been paying attention during practice. Asher played with effortless determination, graceful and efficient. He played intuitively, anticipating his opponent's next move. I hated to admit it, but he played better than me.

But that just made me want it more! And I knew I'd made the right decision to join my dad's team. They played at a higher level, forcing me to up my intensity. Every day I improved my skills, learned something new, or performed in a way I didn't know I could.

Voices rose from downstairs again and then nothing. I held my breath, waiting until Payton's feet pounded on the steps, before opening my door.

Payton's shoulders hunched as he stomped down the hall toward his room. I reached out, stopping short of touching him as he passed me.

"Pay-"

"Leave me alone, Jord." My heart broke at the defeated tone in his voice.

He turned into his room while I watched, wishing I knew what to do with my little brother to make him stop breaking our parents' hearts.

"Love you," I called out, just as he slammed his door shut behind him.

No longer hungry, I abandoned my dinner in favor of a shower. I should honestly shower before dinner, but Mom knew how hungry we all were as soon as we got home and always had dinner on the table. The boys showered at the rink, so I was the only sweaty one most nights or I don't think she'd have been okay with me waiting. One stinky person, she could handle, four of us would have been overwhelming.

I took my shower and returned to my room to get dressed. As I pulled on a pair of gym shorts and an over-sized t-shirt that once belonged to one of my older brothers, I debated if I should keep eavesdropping on Asher.

Whom did it hurt? He didn't know anyone listened. Would he care if he knew? Maybe he should stay inside if he didn't want anyone to hear. Right?

Unable to resist, I grabbed my government textbook and lifted the window before sitting on the beanbag chair I'd hauled up from the basement just for this purpose.

Like clockwork, Asher's voice floated through my open window. For the last few days, he'd been working on the same song. I'd come to conclude what I heard every night was him in the actual process of writing songs. Even though he repeated snippets of the same song over and over again, I never seemed to tire of hearing him sing.

Tonight, however, he started something new. A haunting melody coupled with powerful lyrics about misunderstandings, lost dreams, and wishes on stars.

My government book lay unopened on my lap as Asher's song slipped through my open window and wrapped itself around my heart.

I might be determined not to like the boy, but that didn't mean I couldn't love his song.

Asher

By the start of the third week of school, I'd begun to feel better about moving. My classes running smooth. I'd made a few friends. Joined a band. And I hadn't had any negative interaction with Jordan. I hadn't had any interaction with Jordan at all. And if I were honest, that lack represented the only blemish on an otherwise bright outlook.

Jarom talked to Ms. Jackson about practicing during lunch and advising twice a week, which ironically we had with Ms. Jackson, who fully supported our desire to spend the period working in a practice room.

Until Friday, when she called me over to her desk.

"Hey, Asher. I've been looking over your transcript and realized we need to go over a few things. Why don't you pull a chair around so you can see the computer screen?"

I did as she asked, rolling a chair from the bottom tier to sit behind her desk.

"So, here's a copy of your transcript." A table appeared on the screen with my name at the top. She scrolled down to the end of the table and stopped. "This list at the bottom is everything you still need to do to graduate. You can see you still needed a math class, language arts, government, and science."

"Looks about right. Is there a problem?" Glancing away from the list on the screen, I caught Ms. Jackson staring at me. I smiled. She glanced away, clearing her throat. I tried not to let it go to my head when her cheeks turned pink. She wasn't the first teacher to blush in front of me.

Not wanting to embarrass her any further, I focused on the screen, giving her a chance to collect herself.

She cleared her throat again. "Yes."

Great.

"What is it?"

Mr. Jackson smiled firmly back in teacher mode. "You see, Lakeview participates in a program in conjunction with a non-profit organization that strives to teach students more than just academics. I talked with Mr. Allen, the principal, about the requirements for you since you're already a senior and everyone else has been working on this since freshman year. He agreed to let you complete this packet." She handed me a stapled sheaf of papers.

I flipped through it.

"Don't worry. None of it is graded. You just have to do it. And it shouldn't be hard, but if you do have any trouble, I can help you or any of your other teachers. All your classmates have had to do them as well, so you can get help from them if you need it."

Time-consuming busywork. Perfect. I didn't have much choice, though.

"Okay, that's fine. I'll work on it. Is there a due date?"

Ms. Jackson shook her head. "No, just as long as it's done by graduation. But I wouldn't put it off. Chances are you really won't be in the mood to work on it this spring."

I smiled. "Right. Good advice." I put the packet into my backpack, prepared to not look at it again until absolutely necessary. "Thanks-"

"Oh, wait," she stopped me, her face turning red again. "I'm sorry. The packet is only part of it."

Awesome. I sat back in the chair and waited.

Ms. Jackson cleared her throat, something I realized she did when she was nervous. "Another part of the program requires a certain number of hours of community service-"

My eyes bulged. Community service? What the hell!

Ms. Jackson noticed my expression and hurried to reassure me. "It's not as bad as it sounds, I promise. And I have a project in mind I think you might enjoy."

"Okay, what is it?" I didn't want to be a jerk but come on. Community service? Wasn't that for delinquents?

"It's mentorship for a student over at the middle school. You would go over there during your flex period twice a week and share your talent for music."

Music didn't sound so bad. "So, I'd what? Teach guitar or something?"

Ms. Jackson nodded. "Yeah, if you want. Or you could sing. Piano. Whatever the two of you decide. As long as you provide a positive role model with a focus on music. Twice a week for the semester. You'd have all your hours finished before Christmas. How does that sound?"

"Perfect." I rose from the desk, ready to join the guys in the practice room, and forget all about Ms. Jackson and graduation requirements and lose myself in making music. "Thanks, Ms. Jackson, that sounds kind of fun." Or at least better than picking up garbage on the highway.

She stood up as well. "Great. I still need to meet with someone from the middle school to determine which kids will participate in the program. I'll let you know when I know. How does that sound?"

"Sounds good. Thanks again," I said and then made my way to the practice room.

Jarom, Adam, and Bash worked on one of my songs. Once they found out I wrote my music, they begged to hear some of it. We'd chosen three to begin working on together, adding harmony and including percussion. Jarom had the idea to work on a few songs until we had them the way we wanted them, then put them up on YouTube. I didn't know about all that, but I loved how the first song sounded once we put it all together.

"Man, this sounds so good," Adam said when I walked in.

"I can't believe you aren't already doing gigs." Bash shook his head from behind his drum set. "What's holding you back?"

"I told you guys, my dad." I slung my guitar strap over my shoulder and played the first chords of the song they'd been working on while I talked to Ms. Jackson. "I like what you did with that last part, Adam. Let's start at the top. I want to hear it again. I had an idea."

Happy to not discuss my dad and his lack of support for my passion, I went right into the song.

"Whoa, that sounded so much better." Jarom held out his knuckles.

I tapped them with mine. "We practice a few more times like that and then I say we record it."

"This is going to be so epic," Jarom said.

I didn't think so at first, but now, I kind of thought he might be right.

After school, I found myself walking slowly toward the exit. I hadn't tested Jordan's patience by parking in her spot again, but since I had to take my guitar case in every day, I tried to arrive early enough to get a close space. That morning, the place beside Jordan had been available, and I'd taken it.

My eyes scanned the sea of heads bobbing down the hall toward the door leading to the student parking lot for her particular shade of blonde. Since the incident at practice with Leo, I'd told myself Jordan didn't want anything to do with me. I needed to leave her alone. Easier said than done since I'd become a bit obsessed with a certain tomboy.

Finally, I saw her several feet in front of me and quickened my pace until nobody separated us. I followed her out the door to the parking lot where the noise from the hall dissipated, and a quiet sound reached my ear.

CHAPTER SIX

Jordan

I'd fallen asleep the night before with Asher's song stuck in my head. At different times during the day, I'd caught myself humming the tune, a happy little distraction from the turmoil I'd been experiencing worrying about my little brother. Thank goodness for Friday!

With Asher's melody running through my mind, I burst through the double doors, immediately shedding some of the tension I'd been carrying around since the night before.

"Hey!" Asher's voice, accompanied by his hand on my shoulder, pulled me to a stop in the middle of the school parking lot.

"What's your problem?" I asked, glaring at his hand me.

He dropped it as though I'd burned him. "I'm sorry. I'm sorry. I shouldn't have grabbed you like that. I was just-" He ran his fingers through his hair.

"Just what?" He'd scared the crap out of me, grabbing me like that out of nowhere.

"You were humming," he said.

I rolled my eyes and moved out of the flow of traffic leaving the parking lot toward my car. "That's a federal offense or something?" I said over my shoulder.

Asher pressed his lips into a thin line and followed me. "No, but piracy is. You were humming my tune. I want to know where you heard it."

Oh.

Crap.

Heat flooded my cheeks. My neck. My whole body. I busied myself with putting my backpack in my car while I tried to come up with something to say.

"I, um, how do you know I didn't just make it up?" I squeezed my eyes shut with my back to him and hoped he wouldn't press me.

"Because I listened for more than a couple of bars, Jordan. You hummed the entire first verse and chorus of the song I wrote in my backyard last night."

I opened my eyes to find him standing in front of me, hands on his hips.

I bit my lip.

"Mind explaining how that's possible?" he asked.

He'd caught me. I'd have to tell him the truth. But how? And how humiliating. Why had I never considered the eventuality of this moment?

"Uh," I stuttered.

Asher hooked his thumbs in his belt loops and waited, one brow lifted, for me to explain myself.

Furiously, I tried to come up with something less stalker-ish than *I listen to you sing every night through my open bedroom window, sometimes in a towel.*

I settled for, "I heard you."

His mouth dropped open. "What? How could you have heard me?" His eyes widened as though he'd just thought of something. "Were you spying on me?"

Oh, gosh! It sounded so terrible when he said it like that!

I closed my eyes and shook my head. "No," I hedged. "Not really."

He stared at me, clearly perplexed. "Not really? What does that even mean?"

My cheeks burned as though they'd been dipped in lava.

"I live in the house behind you," I blurted.

Asher opened his mouth and then closed it again before changing his mind one more time and asking, "You what?"

This sucked so bad!

I repeated what I'd told him. "I live in the house behind you." And since he still seemed a bit confused, I continued. "My bedroom faces the backyard."

His mouth snapped shut. He regarded me for a long, awkward moment.

"I'm sorry," I blurted again. Actually... "I'm not sorry I listened to you." His eyes narrowed. "I'm just sorry for listening without your permission."

He didn't say anything for so long, I suddenly became aware of where we were. The parking lot had thinned considerably in the time we'd been talking. Most of the remaining cars belonged to athletes who stayed for practice. Only a handful of people still walked to their cars. Everyone else had already left.

"Let me get this straight. You live," he paused until I met his gaze again. "In the house behind mine, and you what?"

I waited for him to fill in the blank or at least offer me some options, but he didn't. Instead, he just stood there, his brows lifted expectantly.

I decided to give in to my embarrassing fate. "It was an accident, hearing you the first time. I'd just gotten out of the shower," his lips parted just the slightest bit. I could have probably left that particular detail out of my story. Whatever. "My room was hot, and I opened the window. That's when I heard you playing your guitar."

"When was this?"

"The first day of school," I whispered.

He blinked. "And you've been listening," he left the question open.

"Pretty much every day while I do my homework," I admitted, my cheeks blazing with the heat of the sun.

Slowly, so very slowly, his impossibly long lashes lowered to his cheeks before lifting again. "You've been listening to me sing every night without me knowing?"

I nodded, the movement jerky. He had every right to be upset. I'd invaded his privacy by eavesdropping. I should have closed my window when I heard him that first time and resisted the temptation every day after.

My heart raced as I waited for him to say something. Anything.

Our gazes held for what felt like an eternity. Asher's expression went from angry to curious to something else entirely.

My heart beat faster.

His perfect features softened, one side of his mouth lifted. He stepped so close our bodies brushed. I thought about backing away from him, but my feet wouldn't work.

"I'm flattered," he murmured, his voice low.

Heat flooded my body at his closeness, but I couldn't forget. We weren't friends. "Don't be."

His eyes lit with amusement. "You were humming my song. You must like it."

Liked it? I freaking loved it.

I shook my head. "Lots of annoying songs get stuck in my head." I ticked a few off on my fingers. "*The Song That Never Ends. Let it Go. Gangnam Style*. Anything by Taylor Swift."

His lips twitched. "I like Taylor Swift."

"You would."

Asher chuckled low under his breath and took a step away from me toward his car. "I concede. That round goes to you." He shook his head and chuckled again. "See you at practice."

Asher

I got into my car, hoping I appeared more confident than I felt. *Jordan had been listening to me sing?* Every night? She lived in the house behind ours? My mind raced with the implications. The possibilities. Hell, I'd never fall asleep in my bed again knowing she slept less than a hundred yards away.

And what about my evening jam session? Would I be able to play wondering if she listened? She had no idea the effect she had on me. I hadn't been able to stop thinking about the idea of us together since the moment I laid eyes on her. Now, I knew we were neighbors, and she'd been listening to me sing and play. All I wanted was the chance to show her what could be.

But would she give me that chance?

I laughed to myself again. Jordan wanted to like me, I knew it. But she wouldn't let herself.

Why?

Did she hold it against me? That first couple of days when I parked in her spot? Did she hold a grudge because of that day at practice when I mistakenly tried to defend her from that jerk, Leo? He still bugged her at school. I wanted to pound him.

I parked at the rink and hurried inside to change. Coach Parks took practice seriously. His teams won because he made them put in the work. I've always worked hard at hockey. I had to, or I'd have to answer to my dad. Maybe I needed to not worry about Jordan. Or girls in general. I had school, hockey, my music, not to mention Jarom's band. Adding a relationship seemed kind of crazy. Not that it even was an issue.

Should I give up on her? Call me romantic, but I believed in relationships. Love. And while I'd never lacked for female attention, no one had ever made me feel the way Jordan did.

I tried to ignore her during practice, but she didn't make it easy. I loved watching her skate. I couldn't get enough of how tough she played. Jarom hadn't been kidding, Jordan was hella intimidating.

Still, neither of us needed the attention we'd draw if I gave in to the temptation to skate beside her during drills. I'd want to flirt with her.

I snorted to myself. Her dad and brother would appreciate that, for sure. I couldn't risk my position on the team by ticking them off because I had the hots for Jordan.

Didn't keep my eyes from finding her, however. Her blonde ponytail made her easy to spot. She played with intensity, her passion for the game evident every time she stepped onto the ice. What she lacked in stature, she made up for with quickness and stealth.

Of course, Jordan had already left by the time I reached my car in the parking lot. We didn't live far from the rink, but this time instead of turning down our street, I took the road before it, curious to see where exactly Jordan lived. Sure enough, her beat-up car sat in the driveway of the house directly behind mine.

What were the odds?

Not wanting to get caught behaving like a stalker, I continued home. Shari's mom-mobile and Dad's sleek sports car took up the driveway, so I parked on the street.

"How was practice?" Shari asked with a bright smile when I walked into the kitchen.

"Good," I replied with a smile at Caleb, who sat in his high chair. His little feet kicked and his hands waved as he blew spit bubbles at the sight of me. What a cute kid.

"Can I get him out?" I always asked if she had him strapped into something. Sometimes picking him up when he was content just made him mad.

"Sure," Shari said.

"Come here, bud." Caleb's limbs flailed furiously the closer I got, and when I held out my arms, he started doing this squealing thing he did when he got excited.

"He's glad to see you," Shari laughed, shaking her head at him.

"I'm glad to see him, too." I blew a raspberry on Caleb's neck making him giggle, so I did it again. His hands slapped at my cheeks. "Ow!" I yelped. "I'm gonna get you for that." I tucked one of his arms under mine and held the other with my hand then tickled his belly with my face. Caleb's body writhed as he laughed.

"That's torture!" Shari poked my ribs. I jumped out of her reach. "You don't like being tickled!"

At all. I hated being tickled. But Caleb loved it. Even though he squirmed to get away from me when I tickled him, he'd get mad if I stopped.

"He loves it," I told her before nuzzling his fleshy neck with my chin. I could listen to my little brother giggle all day long, he was so cute. "I can let him crawl around my room for a bit while you finish dinner," I offered. Caleb liked getting into all my stuff, and I didn't mind having him around.

"That would be great. Just make sure he doesn't put anything in his mouth," she warned.

"Don't worry. I've Caleb-proofed my room." And I'd recheck the floor before putting him down.

"Alright, then. Thanks, Asher." Shari turned back to dinner prepa-rations while I hauled Caleb up to my room and shut the door. If I didn't, he'd crawl out and try to fall down the stairs. He and I had been working on going down backward, but sometimes he still tried to go down head first, and that was a visit to the hospital waiting to happen.

"Okay, bud, here you go." I set him on the carpet with a few of his toys from the last time he came to visit my room and a handful of things he probably shouldn't have like my magic 8-ball and the remote to my television, but he loved to play with them, and I made sure to keep an eye on him.

"Ba!" Caleb shouted, bringing both fists down at his sides.

"Okay, okay, sheesh," I muttered as I rolled the 8-ball across the short distance between us on the carpet. He picked it up and immedi-ately brought it to his mouth. It was too big to fit, of course, so he just slobbered all over it, but I didn't care.

Caleb and I played with his toys for a little while, but then he got distracted with a pile of socks (they were clean!), so I wandered over to my window. My bedroom sat on the corner at the back of the house. It had two windows, one facing the side yard and one facing the back. Standing by the one facing the backyard, I could see the house behind ours, the one where Jordan lived. She said her bedroom faced her back-yard, and I took a few minutes to study each of the three windows on the upper level of the Parks' house. One was a bathroom. It had frosted glass and was too small to be a bedroom. But the other two were similar enough I had no idea which one might be Jordan's.

Since she told me where she lived, I'd been thinking of a way to get her to hang out with me. I doubted it would be as simple as asking her, so I needed a plan. And hopefully, the one I'd come up with would work.

CHAPTER SEVEN

Jordan

Nothing like another tense evening in the Parks household. Payton didn't look up once as he made quick work of his dinner before escaping to his room as soon as possible. After helping Mom clean up the dinner dishes, I did the same thing. I'd only had a few math problems for homework and finished them during advising. With no homework to distract me, I caught myself dwelling on the conversation I'd had with Asher in the parking lot after school more than I wanted to.

Beyond the embarrassment of getting caught humming the song he'd been playing in his backyard the night before, I didn't know what to think about the way he made me feel. There was no use denying I wanted him to kiss me, but every time I thought about giving in to the attraction I felt, I remembered my rule and why it existed in the first place.

Think about it. Why did people always say you shouldn't date your boss? Or your brother's best friend? Or the nanny? Because it put something important on the line. A job. A friendship. A child's wellbeing. Same thing with dating a teammate. It put the team on the line, brought romantic drama where there shouldn't be. I had a dream to play competitive hockey at the highest level. Playing for my dad gave me the best shot. The kinds of feelings I had for Asher threatened everything I'd been working for.

Wait.

Tilting my head, I strained my ears to listen.

What was that?

Jordan, Jordan.
I know you can hear me.
Why won't you come near me?
I'm writing this song for you-ooh, ooh.

My entire body flared with heat. He kept singing. I had to bite my lip to keep from grinning.

I'm gonna keep singing this ridiculous song
Until you come outside and sing along.

"Come on, Jordan!" he shouted.

I closed my eyes. Someone would hear him. No part of me wanted anyone in my house to hear him singing to me from the backyard. But how to get him to stop?

Jordan, Jordan.
I know you can hear me.
But what about your dad?
Don't you think he'll be mad?

For goodness sake! I moved to the window. Asher stood under my window, grinning like a fool.

"Do all your songs rhyme?" I called down.

"You know they don't, you little eavesdropper. Now, come down here!" He kept plucking at his guitar, watching me.

I bit my lip as his smile widened.

"You know you want to!"

He was right. I did want to. What could possibly go wrong in my own backyard? I'd just go down there, hang out for a few minutes, and then make up some excuse to leave. Like I had to finish my homework. Or wash my hair.

"Alright, alright. I'll be down in a second. Just be quiet." Using both hands, I closed the window. I'd thrown on leggings and a fitted tee after my shower, so I tossed a hoodie over my head, then slipped into a pair of flip-flops. My hair was a hopeless mess after my shower. I settled for running a brush through it, then taming it into a ponytail.

"Where you headed?" Dad asked as soon as I rounded the corner at the bottom of the stairs. He sat on the sectional in front of the television, Mom curled at his side.

"Just out back," I replied, praying he wouldn't ask any more questions.

Dad frowned a little, but he didn't say anything. I decided to hurry before he changed his mind. Or went to investigate.

Outside, Asher paced the grass between our houses, his guitar hanging around his middle as he picked different notes from the strings. He mumbled words and phrases, but when he turned and spotted me, a happy grin split his handsome face. He laughed as his fingers played the melody I'd been humming earlier when he caught me.

"Oh, stop!" I called out playfully, but his smile only grew.

"What? I thought you liked this song," he teased me.

"I never said that."

He laughed again. "Whatever. You know you do."

It would take a lot more than his teasing to get me to admit it, though.

"If this is just going to be you fishing for compliments," I raised my voice to sound like a groupie, "*Oh, Asher, you're such a good singer, swoon!*" I rolled my eyes and spoke in my normal voice. "Then, I'll just go back inside."

"No, no, don't go." He grabbed hold of my wrist, pulling me back around. "And please, don't ever talk like that again. Let's just go into my office and chat for a little while." He pulled me toward a set of wrought iron patio furniture in a cluster of low bushes at the base of a shade tree in his yard.

I raised one brow. "This is your office?"

He dropped my hand and sighed as he glanced around. "I know. It's a little sparse, and the furniture makes my butt fall asleep, but it is what it is." He pointed to the single chair across from a narrow loveseat. "Sit. Please."

I took the chair he indicated while Asher sat in the center of the love seat, propping his guitar on his knee. His fingers plucked at the strings almost absently, his attention focused solely on me.

"I'm glad you came down."

"You didn't give me much choice." Glancing at the ground near his feet, I noticed a handful of guitar picks littering the grass. I bent down to pick one up, holding it in the space between us. "Lose something?"

His fingers squeaked on the strings before he reached for it. "All the time. I have about a hundred of them up in my room."

"You don't use them all the time?" I asked.

He shook his head as he began to play again, this time using the pick. "No. Listen." He played and I did indeed listen, fascinated by the sound, even more beautiful close up than it had been drifting through my window. If that were possible.

"Now, listen to this." He tucked the guitar pick between his teeth and played using just his fingers. The motions were subtly different, but I did hear it.

He glanced up at me. "Hear it?"

I nodded. "How long have you been playing?"

"My dad said I was born with a guitar in my hands. I don't have any memories of not being able to play."

"What, are you like some prodigy?" How did a little kid learn how to play the guitar?

Asher laughed, and it struck me anew how much I liked his appearance.

"No, not at all. My mom," he gave me a look, "my biological mom, she's talented. My dad says I'm a lot like her."

"Your biological mom?"

"Yeah, my parents divorced when I was two." He started picking out a melody I hadn't heard before. I tried to imagine what it would be like to have songs in my head.

"So, you live with your dad?"

He nodded. "And my step-mom, Shari."

"Do you have any siblings?"

"A little brother, Caleb. He's ten months old."

"A baby?"

Asher grinned. "You like babies?"

I scoffed. "Who doesn't like babies?"

He reached into his pocket and pulled out his phone. After a couple of taps, he handed it to me. "Here's a picture."

"Oh my gosh! He's so cute." The picture showed a tiny baby, younger than ten months, propped on a pair of legs I assumed were Asher's.

"Scroll through. I have a million." He started playing again, and I thought he did it without even thinking.

I scrolled through his pictures. He hadn't been lying. There were a lot of pictures of Caleb and quite a few with Asher, too, selfies of him making faces for the camera and Caleb laughing.

I stopped on one of Caleb playing in a toilet, grinning adorably. Lifting one brow, I tilted it toward Asher.

"Hey!" he cried, trying to take the phone away from me as I held it out of his reach. "I forgot that was on there. Shari would kill me if she saw it. I was supposed to be watching him when that happened."

"You were babysitting and let him play in the toilet?" Shaking my head, I made a tsk-ing sound with my tongue as I studied the picture again.

"I got distracted, okay? And I totally bathed him and even brushed his three teeth to be on the safe side. I've learned my lesson, too. I'm an amazing babysitter now."

I scrolled through a couple more pictures before giving Asher his phone back. "He's adorable."

Asher slipped his phone back into his pocket. "He is," he said, his dark eyes meeting mine, holding me captive. "But I think we need to talk about your eavesdropping some more."

Asher

The need to tease her had become irresistible. She liked listening to me sing and play, I knew she did. And it was intoxicating.

"It's not eavesdropping," she said, her cheeks turning pink. "You play outside where the whole world can hear you."

"Hmmm. I guess that's true," I replied before slipping into the lyrics of the song I'd written a long time ago about friends, and love, and loss. I never took my eyes away from her as I sang.

I played the last note. Silence hung between us.

"Did you write that?"

I nodded, desperately wishing she'd tell me what she thought. I kind of felt like I knew she liked my music— why would she have listened for so long if she didn't— but I still wanted to hear her say it. Maybe someday.

"You're good, you know."

She made a face. "What are you talking about? I can't sing or play the guitar."

I grinned. "No, that's not what I meant." I cleared my throat. "I mean hockey."

Her open expression closed a little, and I felt a twinge of panic. I didn't want her to leave. I didn't want to make her angry, either.

She shrugged. "I'm okay."

"Okay?" I scoffed. "Jordan, you're amazing." I didn't say it just to say it. "I mean it."

She met my gaze with a direct one of her own. "Not as good as you."

I didn't deny it because she told the truth. "You want it more."

For a long moment, she held my eyes, searching for some truth. If she asked me, I'd tell her. Right then, I knew I'd tell her anything.

Finally, she found what she'd been looking for. "Hockey isn't your passion." A statement.

I shook my head. "No." Notes began to form in my mind, a pattern I wanted to explore. My fingers moved, creating the sound in my head.

Jordan watched, mesmerized for a moment before she snapped out of it. "But you like it? Hockey?"

I shrugged. "I don't hate it." I just didn't love it enough. I had to push myself, motivated only by my music. "My dad wants me to play."

Jordan frowned.

And I had a feeling I knew exactly what went through her head. In all probability, I'd start in our first game. And she'd play off the bench. She'd have playing time, lots of it, but my size and strength paired with my knowledge of the game surpassed her combined abilities.

I would take her spot and I didn't even want to play. I saw it the moment it dawned on her.

She jumped up.

I scrambled to my feet. "Jordan, wait!"

She'd made it almost to her back door before I caught up to her.

"Look, I'm sorry!"

She whirled around to face me, her expression murderous. "You're better than me. Fine. That's my problem, not yours. I'm not afraid to work. But you don't even want it?"

What could I say? She was right.

"You don't make it to this level for fun, Asher. Everyone on that team is there because they want it."

I heard what she said. She wanted it. To go on and play at the highest level she could achieve.

"You don't understand." I would quit the team right that very minute if I could. My dad assumed I'd change my mind once I had a taste of winning and develop a competitive streak. Nothing I said would change his mind. I'd just have to prove him wrong. Until then, as he loved to remind me, I lived under his roof, drove his car, ate his food. And for all that, I had to keep playing hockey.

Even if it meant robbing Jordan of her dream.

When I graduated high school, everything would be different. I wouldn't be under his thumb, wouldn't have to live by his rules.

"You're right. I don't understand. You don't get to this level of play without expectations, Asher. It's not just me. It's everyone on the team. We all have the dream to play professional hockey."

What she didn't say— my being on the team took that shot away from someone else who wanted it. Someone like her, even though she was already on the team.

"It's more complicated than that. My dad-" I broke off. She didn't need to know all my secrets. "It's just...complicated."

Jordan shook her head. "Seems simple to me."

She wasn't being fair. "You don't know everything."

"You're right. I don't know you." And then she walked away.

Damn it!

Brimming with frustration, I turned away from her. It was easy for her to judge! She'd been doing nothing but sorting me into boxes since we met. Stalking up to the house, I whipped the back door open, then slammed it shut once I made it inside.

"Asher!" Shari looked up, her eyes wide. "What's the matter?"

"Nothing," I answered, heading for the stairs.

"Who was that girl you were talking to?" she called.

"Nobody!" I shouted over my shoulder.

Nobody.

The biggest lie of them all.

In two weeks, I'd fallen into the deepest crush I'd ever experienced in my life for a girl who hated my guts.

CHAPTER EIGHT

Jordan

For the next week, I avoided Asher as much as possible. I didn't open my window, didn't listen to him practice his music, and more than anything else, I didn't search for him in the halls at school.

Okay. Maybe I did. But only because I couldn't help myself. Something about him drew me against my will. It could have been those pictures of him with his little brother. Or maybe his good looks. Or even the depth of feeling in his song lyrics. Whatever it was, I wanted to ignore it. I wanted to push it away, push him away.

Worst of all, I'd come to the conclusion I had no right to be angry with him. He'd made the team. I couldn't blame him for being a better player. My failures were just that, my own. Realizing my anger came from pride made me angry...at myself.

Which didn't help my attitude. At all.

Finally, Friday rolled around again. One more day of practice before the weekend. The next day both Natalie and Kelly had sports in town. I planned to spend the day watching my friends compete while trying to forget all about Asher, his song, and how much I didn't want to like him.

Once school ended, I hurried out to my car and shoved the key into the ignition.

Nothing.

"What?" I murmured and tried again. No dice.

Crap. Now, what was I going to do? I could call Joe, but he lived on the other side of town. Mom should be at home, but who knew. She could be out running errands. Dad would already be at the rink by now.

I pulled my phone from my pocket and scrolled through my favorites folder until Joe's name popped up. My thumb hovered over the call button when a knock sounded on my window.

Asher.

Of course.

I gave him a *what do you want?* face. He lifted his brow as if to say *isn't it obvious*. I waved for him to open the door.

"What are you doing? Is something wrong?" he asked as soon as he opened the door.

"My car won't start."

He sat down in the passenger side seat and frowned. "Try to start it."

I turned the key in the ignition. "See? Nothing."

"Want to jump it? We can use my car, but I don't have any cables."

Ugh. "I don't, either. I think they might be in Joe's car." He'd gotten himself a used car before he moved out. A couple of months ago, his battery kept dying, so he'd held onto the jumper cables. I'd never had an issue with this car, so I hadn't been worried about it.

Asher checked the time on his phone. "We're going to be late if we don't hurry. I'll give you a ride, then you can let your dad know about your car."

Without waiting to see what I'd say, he got out of my car. He paused before closing the door to glance back at me.

"Coming?"

Practice started in just a few minutes. Chances were Joe had already arrived at the rink. Asher had to be at the same place as me. Refusing the ride would be silly.

But that didn't mean I wanted to get into his car. At. All.

"Jordan, come on. We're going to the same place." His dark eyes held mine. "What are you afraid of?"

Nothing. I wasn't afraid of anything.

I grabbed my bag and marched to his car. Before I could sit down, our eyes met over the roof.

"What?" I asked with more irritation than he deserved considering he'd saved me from having to call Joe or wait for my mom.

One side of his mouth curved up. "Nothing. Let's go."

I plopped down on the soft leather covering the front seat, my head falling back against the headrest. His car still had a new car smell. It was so clean my cheeks heated thinking of him sitting in our junker with fast food wrappers and dirty socks on the floor, even if it had only been for a moment.

His long fingers pushed a button to start the car. Fancy. He pulled out of the parking lot and turned in the direction of the rink.

"So..." He shifted in his seat. "How's it going?"

I rolled my head to the side and glared at him. "Fine. And you?"

His lips twitched. "Fine." He glanced away from the road to look at me for a split second. "Heard any good music lately?"

"No. Not really."

He laughed. "Fair enough." He turned down a side street to avoid the stoplights on the main road. "How are your friends? What are their names?" His eyes squinted. "Natalie and Kelly?"

"They're fine."

Asher stopped at a stop sign. "Good talk. We should do this again sometime."

I rolled my head again, this time to look out the window while I pondered a witty comeback. Instead, I saw~

"Wait! Stop the car!" If I hadn't been so determined to avoid Asher's gaze, I might have missed it, missed *him.*

"What? What are you talking about?"

Too afraid to turn away from the window, I blindly reached for his forearm and squeezed. "Please. Just pull over." I pointed to an empty spot on the curb. "Right there. Hurry!"

To his credit, Asher didn't ask any more questions as he maneuvered his car to the side of the road and parked.

"What's going on?" he asked, but I didn't have time for stupid questions.

Yanking on the handle, I burst through the car door. "Payton!" Not even bothering to close the door, I took off running after my brother. "Payton!"

Asher

What the hell?

Scrambling from the car, I ran after her, slamming her door shut on the way. "Jordan!"

She ran down an alley between a row of houses.

"Payton!" she cried.

Searching ahead, I spotted a group of four middle school kids. All boys. One of them glanced up when Jordan called out, his brows lifting with surprise before lowering again. Scowling, he turned to his friends and said something before striding toward Jordan.

I stopped a couple of yards away.

"Jordan, what are you doing here?" The kid stood with his shoulders hunched, fists clenched at his sides.

"No, what are you doing here? You're supposed to be at practice."

The kid, Payton, glanced over his shoulder at his friends. He turned back to Jordan, his face twisted with anger.

"How do you know I'm not on my way there?" he asked.

Jordan put her hands on her hips. "I'm not stupid, Payton. The rink is on the other side of the middle school from here." She pointed to his friends. "They aren't on your team."

Payton scowled. "Butt out, Jordan. It's none of your business what I'm doing." His gaze flicked over me. "Just get back in the car with your boyfriend and leave me alone." He started to turn away, but

Jordan grabbed his arm. My body tensed, ready to help if she needed me.

"He's not my boyfriend, and you're coming with me." She pulled on his arm, but the kid dug in his heels.

"No, I'm not." He shot another look at his friends. One of them laughed, making catcalls.

Jordan stopped pulling but didn't let go of his arm. "Dad is going to kill you when he finds out you skipped hockey practice." She lowered her voice, but I heard what she said. "You're already in enough trouble. What's wrong with you?"

Payton's scowl deepened as my gaze darted between the two siblings. "What's it to you? Go away, Jordan."

Jordan's jaw dropped. "What's it to me? You're my brother! Do you think it's fun being sent away from dinner to sit in my room while you get yelled at?"

Payton's jaw clenched, his face turning red. His friends had quieted down again, waiting to see what he'd do next. I stepped forward as Payton leaned toward Jordan, his nose barely an inch from hers.

"Leave. Me. Alone." He wrenched his arm from her grasp and took off running, his friends following close behind, their laughter echoing down the alley.

Jordan started after him, but I caught her, wrapping my arms around her waist from behind.

"Let him go," I said as she struggled against my hold.

"No! That's my brother!" Jordan's hair whipped in my face. I tightened my grip.

"I know. What are you going to do? Chase him down? Then what? You can't make him do something he doesn't want to do."

She struggled a few seconds more before her body sagged against mine. "Dad's going to kill him."

"No, he won't. And even if he is mad, that's on Payton. Not you."

Jordan turned in my arms and buried her face in my chest. "I don't know why he's doing this! He's not a bad kid." She tilted her face until our eyes met. "Did you see those kids?" she asked, eyes watering.

I nodded, knowing exactly what she meant and having no right to judge. Anyone looking at me could lump me in with those kids. Dark clothes. Shaggy hair. Bad attitude. Give them a guitar, put them in a band-

"He's been in trouble for months," the words spilled from her mouth. "He was grounded most of the summer because he got caught driving his friend's mom's car at two in the morning. He got pulled over by the police." She shook her head. I could almost feel her pain, her worry. "It was horrible. Mom and Dad had to pick him up at the police station. If he's not careful, he's going to end up in juvie." Her voice broke on the last word. Her face dropped to my chest again as quiet sobs wracked her body. I had a feeling Jordan Parks didn't cry over much. Her brother was breaking her heart.

Not knowing what else to do and not minding having her close, I tucked her head under my chin and just held on until she'd cried all she could cry.

"I'm sorry," she whispered into my shirt.

"Don't be." Her arms went slack around my waist, my cue to let her go.

Jordan wiped the tears from her cheeks with her hands. "Gah! What's the matter with me?" She gave me her back and continued to scrub at her face. "I just cried all over a stranger!"

I tried not to let her words hurt because I knew what she meant. "I'm not that strange. You did eavesdrop on me singing."

Jordan whirled around, her cheeks blazing. "I-" She stopped, pointing her finger at me. "That-" Her lips pressed into a flat line as she glared.

"You're incredibly adorable when you're flustered," I said, reaching out to tuck a wisp of her hair behind her ear.

"No, I'm not." She pushed my hand away, making me laugh.

"You are. Come on. We're going to be late to practice."

Her eyes widened. "Practice! Dad is going to kill *us*!"

"Well, then let's go." Grabbing her hand, I pulled her toward my car.

We drove to the rink in silence. Jordan needed time to collect herself and truth be told, so did I. I'd been on this girl's wrong side since the moment she laid eyes on me. First, in the parking lot and during lunch on the first day of school. Then, at practice. She'd been avoiding me. Glaring at me. Fearing I would somehow steal her dream of starting. I understood that kind of fear, had experienced it myself. Jordan's passion for hockey matched my own for music.

Somehow, I hoped we'd both get what we wanted.

As soon as I turned off the engine, we launched out of our seats to grab our gear. Fifteen minutes late. We sprinted across the parking lot. I reached out to hold the door for her. Inside, the sound of Coach's whistle echoed in the halls as he called out drills.

"Don't worry about Dad. Once I explain everything, he won't be mad." She gave me a sad look. "At least, not at us."

I nodded, not knowing what to say. We arrived at the guy's locker room first. I stopped while Jordan kept going. For some reason, instead of rushing inside to change, I stood there, watching her.

She'd almost made it to the women's locker room when she paused and turned around. I hadn't moved. She didn't seem surprised to find me still there.

"Thank you, Asher." The sincerity in her voice made my heart skip a beat. Could this be my chance to be more than Jordan's competition on the ice? More than the guy who annoyed her by parking in her spot and sitting at her lunch table?

"You're welcome."

I didn't know the answer, but I knew what I hoped. I hoped we could start over.

CHAPTER NINE

Jordan

I was right. Dad didn't get mad. At least, not at me. And not at Asher. I'd seen the two of them talking at the end of practice. When they finished, Dad shook Asher's hand and clapped him on the shoulder. Probably thanking him for giving me a ride.

After practice, I rode with Dad to the high school to pick up my car. He didn't say anything about Payton, I already told him everything once Asher and I made it on the ice, but stress and anger made his shoulders and brow tight.

At the school, Dad removed the jumper cables from the back of his SUV while I popped the hood of my car. He connected the cables. Before long, the engine started.

"I'll see you at home," he said once he'd disconnected the cables again.

"Dad-" I started to say, but he cut me off.

"Just go on home, kiddo." His voice sounded tired, worn completely out.

"Okay." I hated feeling this way. I could just strangle my brother for making my parents worry like this!

Dad watched me until I drove out of the parking lot.

When I got home, Mom met me at the door, her eyes red from crying. I knew right away Payton hadn't come back yet. Dad must be out looking for him.

"I warmed up some leftovers," she said while keeping her vigil at the front door.

I couldn't eat. Instead, I headed up the stairs to shower. Once I finished, I opened my window and tried to work on my homework, but found it impossible to concentrate. Who could think about math after a day like today?

Not me.

I abandoned my homework for the beanbag chair under the window. I hadn't been able to bring myself to open my window in days, but tonight, I hoped Asher would be out there. I needed to hear his song.

With my window open, the cool breeze brushing over my skin, I waited. Instead, I heard the front door slam and Dad's angry voice. Mom's softer tones worked to calm him, but Payton yelled over her.

More shouts from downstairs reached my room, and I decided to send a group text to Joe and Bobby. I'd already sent one earlier to let them know Payton had run off.

Me: Dad found him.

Bobby texted back almost immediately. He was in Indianapolis for a game, but wouldn't play until the next night.

Bobby: He getting his butt chewed?

Me: Big time.

Joe chimed in. I hadn't had much of an opportunity to talk to him after practice. Dad had been in a hurry to get out of there.

Joe: What an idiot! What's his problem anyway?

Bobby: Puberty?

Me: Eww.

Joe: *fist bump*

Me: I thought it would be better after the car thing over the summer.

Joe: Kid was scared crapless.

Bobby: He needs something to focus on other than getting in trouble.

Dad said that all the time, find something to focus on to keep busy. It was one of the reasons we all played hockey. He believed it would keep us out of trouble. It worked for the older boys.

Me: Hello. Hockey.

Joe: Pay isn't into it like we are.

True. While Bobby, Joe, and I couldn't get enough of our favorite sport, Payton groaned whenever we put on our rollerblades to play in our basement with brooms and tennis balls. Mom insisted we play with full equipment once we got big enough to hurt each other. When Bobby and Joe lived at home, there were always guys downstairs playing.

Bobby: What's he into then?

Joe: Being a dirtbag.

Me: Super helpful, Joey.

It made me think, though. Fine, Payton didn't love hockey the same as we did. But there had to be something else he felt passionate about. Other than getting in trouble.

Outside my window, Asher plucked his guitar strings, drawing my attention away from my phone, but not away from my brothers completely.

Bobby: We gotta think of something, guys. That little turd's only 12 and he's already been picked up by the police. What's he gonna be like when he gets older?

A sobering thought.

I told my brothers I'd talk to them later. The music outside my window stopped abruptly. I didn't think much of it until it didn't start back up again after several moments. I lifted myself onto my knees, peeking over the window sill into the backyard.

"Bahhh." I fell back onto the beanbag, clutching my chest where my heart raced.

Deep laughter floated into my bedroom through the open window.

"Come down and talk to me."

Holy crap, Jordan!

I peered out the window again. Asher stood just below my window.

"Why would I want to do that?"

He made a face. "Why wouldn't you? Come on."

The memory of his arms around me while I cried asked the same question. Why wouldn't I?

Without replying, I shut my window and tossed on a hoodie. Downstairs, my parents still talked with Payton. They'd moved into the kitchen, blocking me from using the back door. If I wanted to avoid them, I'd have to leave through the front and walk around.

And I did want to avoid them.

Asher waited in our yard, his guitar hanging from a strap around his chest around his back. He didn't say anything. Instead, he opened his arms and for some crazy reason, I walked straight into them.

The only sound in the backyard, other than my out of whack heart, came from inside my house.

"I was worried," he said into my hair. "Did he just get home?"

I nodded, my face pressed against his chest.

Asher sighed. Somehow, I felt glad he'd been the one with me earlier when I found Payton. His calm reassurance differing vastly from the response I'd have gotten from my friends if they'd been the ones with me.

"Let's sit down." Asher let go of me only to slide his hand into mine. He led me to the wrought iron furniture where we sat a week ago. Only this time, he removed his guitar from around his torso and leaned it against the chair before pulling me down beside him on the loveseat. And again, I let him.

"Wanna talk about it?" he asked.

For some crazy reason, I did.

"Payton's twelve. He's the youngest. There's a larger age gap between him and me than between our older two brothers and me. He's always been the baby, you know?" I had no idea why I told him anything, but it didn't matter. He asked, and I needed to vent.

Asher nodded. "Believe me, I understand about the baby in the family."

I smiled a little, thinking about his little brother. "That's right, you do."

Asher sat back, pulling me with him. His arm curled around my shoulders, feeling comfortable, and just...right.

"It's not exactly the same, because Caleb's still a baby, but there's no denying it's not the same for him as it has been for me."

I nodded because he was right. "Well, Payton's always been a little different. I guess it is for me, too, because I'm the only girl, but I've kind of always been one of the guys."

Asher snorted but didn't say anything.

"Anyway, Payton's never been into hockey like the rest of us. He's always been a bit more broody."

Asher's fingers toyed with my hair. Before I could think better of it, I turned my face into him, inhaling deeply, enjoying the spicy scent he wore.

"What does he like to do? Maybe he wouldn't be acting out if he didn't have to play hockey."

Asher

A trace of bitterness laced my words, but I didn't know if Jordan picked up on it or not. I knew all about being forced to do something you didn't want to do. The difference for me, I'd found my passion. As long as I could do both things, I'd compromise.

Maybe if Payton could find the thing he loved, he could work something out that would keep him out of trouble.

To my surprise, Jordan snuggled into my side. I wanted to comment, ask what went on in that beautiful head of hers but feared breaking whatever spell we were under. I didn't want it to end.

"It's crazy you say that. Bobby, Joe, and I were just saying the same thing. But Dad would never let Payton quit hockey. One, he's too good, even if he doesn't like it. Two, hockey's an institution in our family. Everybody plays. My uncles. My cousins. I have an aunt who plays for the US National team."

"Wow. That's cool. But that doesn't mean Payton doesn't have something else he's interested in." Like me, I wanted to say but didn't because we were talking about her brother, not me.

Jordan sat up straight, putting a distance between us I regretted until her hands gripped my arms. The intensity in her gaze had nothing to do with the thoughts running around in my head, but heaven help me, her lips were just inches away.

"You mean like you and your music," she asked.

"Well, yeah."

We'd already discussed hockey wasn't my passion. In fact, that very conversation had been the catalyst leading to a week of complete radio silence from Jordan. She hadn't even been eavesdropping on my nightly jam sessions in my backyard. I knew because I'd been spying on her window. Unless she'd been sly about it, Jordan hadn't been listening to me sing.

Which was fine. I'd been surprised when she said she liked listening in the first place. I just figured her not opening her window meant she was still upset with me. And that kind of sucked.

"Asher," she said, pulling me away from my thoughts and back to the present.

"What?" Man, I wanted to kiss her. I wanted to spend every waking minute with her. What did that mean? I'd never felt this way about anyone before.

"I just thought of something. It might be a long shot, me looking for something that isn't there, but what about music?"

"What about music?" I asked.

Her shoulders fell a little as she rolled her eyes. "For Payton!" She grabbed my hands, further distracting me from the words coming out of her mouth. "He's always got his earbuds in listening to some weird band or another. What if we got him into music?"

"We?" I'd do just about anything Jordan asked me at this point but was she asking?

"What if–" She bit her lip.

"Yeah? What if…"

"Never mind. It's stupid. You're probably busy anyway. I was just thinking..." She shrugged. "I just thought maybe music could help him somehow."

"And you want me to-"

"Nothing. I'm not thinking straight. Why would you want to help some out-of-control middle schooler? That's right. You wouldn't."

Suddenly, all the stars aligned and my brain started working the way it should even though Jordan still had her side pressed against mine, my hands clasped in hers.

"Wait a second." I needed just a little more time to figure this out. "Listen, I have an idea, but I can't guarantee it'll work. If it doesn't, we can try to think of something else, but if we did it this way, I'd for sure have time."

Jordan frowned, obviously not following me. "Can't guarantee what will work?"

"Ms. Jackson talked to me last week about some dumb thing I have to do to graduate. Community service hours or something like that."

Jordan nodded. "Right. We all have to do it. I finished last year." Her eyes widened. "Are they making you do all the hours?"

"I don't know. She just said this semester during flex."

"Oh. That's good. It makes sense they'd cut you some slack since you just moved here." She frowned again. "But what does that have to do with Payton?"

"I'm getting to that. One of the projects she told me about is mentoring kids from the middle school, teaching guitar, talking about music, whatever."

Jordan's eyes lit. "But that's perfect! Do you think they'd let you work with Payton?"

"I don't know, but it's worth a shot to ask."

Jordan squee-ed, an uncharacteristic noise coming from her. "And you'll ask? You'll see if she'll let you mentor Payton?"

"Well, yeah. Of course." Because, as mentioned, I had a feeling I'd do just about anything for this girl and she didn't even know it.

"Thank you!" She threw her arms around my neck. "Thank you." Her voice choked on the last word.

Slowly, tentatively, I put my arms around her waist. "You're welcome. But I haven't done anything yet."

She shook her head, her face glowing. "It doesn't matter. I've been wracking my brain trying to find a way to help him and haven't come up with anything. For the first time in months, I feel hope. Even if this doesn't work out, even if it does and nothing changes, I'll feel better knowing we tried." She hugged me again. "Thank you."

I hugged her in return, inhaling deeply. Who knew when I'd get the chance to hold her again. Jordan's hair smelled fruity and girly. I knew I'd be dreaming about it that night.

All too soon, she pulled back, withdrawing her hands from around my neck. Even in the dim light of dusk, her cheeks were visibly red. I wanted to reassure her she had nothing to be embarrassed about. I wanted to hold her. I wanted to help her. I wanted her.

"I should go," she said, rising to her feet. I scrambled to follow. She took a step to leave and then stopped. "I'll see you tomorrow?"

"Yes." And every day after if she'd allow it.

"Bye, Asher."

I watched as she picked her way across the lawn, exhaling a deep breath while hoping and praying with all my might I wouldn't let this girl down.

CHAPTER TEN

Jordan

Maybe I'd misjudged Asher. Or maybe I'd been too quick to judge because he'd unwittingly threatened my two greatest loves on that first day we met, my family and my game. He still posed a threat on the ice, but after our conversation the night before, I felt more hope than I had in a long time when it came to my family because of him. If Asher could help Payton discover a love of music, maybe he'd stop hanging around kids who were a bad influence. And if that happened? It would be a miracle for our family.

We showed up at school at the same time the next morning.

"You stalking me now?" I asked as he fell into step beside me.

"Absolutely," he answered. "Is that okay? I mean, you did eavesdrop on me for a whole two weeks without my knowledge." He nudged my arm with his elbow.

"You should have stayed inside if you didn't want anyone to hear you." I nudged him back.

"Oh, I don't care that you listened." Without missing a step, he leaned down to murmur in my ear. "It's kinda hot."

Oh, wow. I swallowed hard. But I couldn't let him know how much he affected me.

"Don't get cocky, Sloane. It was either listen to you or listen to my parents chew out my brother."

"Oh-ho!" He held his fist in front of his mouth. "Burn. You are mean."

I patted his arm. "Don't be so sensitive. On second thought, it wasn't that bad. Kind of like getting serenaded every evening."

Asher wrapped his arm around my waist, pulling me around in front of him. He kept us moving, me walking backward with both his arms around me. His dark, heavy-lidded eyes met mine. "Serenaded, huh? That's what it takes to get your attention? Because if so, I'm down."

I bit my lip to hold back my grin. I could get down with flirting with him, but he didn't need to know that.

"Oh, no. It would take a lot more than singing outside my bedroom window to get my attention." I stepped out of his hold and left him standing in the middle of the sidewalk. "See you later."

"What the heck was that?" Natalie came out of nowhere, or maybe I'd been too distracted by Asher to notice her. "I thought we hated him?"

"We do," I said.

"Uh-huh. You keep telling yourself that, Jord."

"He's doing me a favor."

Natalie lifted a brow.

I pushed her shoulder. "Not like that. Get your mind out of the gutter."

"Hey, you were the one hugging him."

"Who hugged who?" Kelly asked as she joined us.

"Jordan and Asher," Natalie said.

Kelly's eyes widened. "I thought you couldn't stand that guy. Are you guys going out now?"

"What? No. Absolutely not." I shook my head, back and forth.

Natalie nudged Kelly. "They were hugging for like a long time."

"Really?" Kelly's eyes lit. "You like him!"

"I do not!" Ugh. I hated my friends right now. "He's helping me-"

"Right. Helping you." Natalie winked.

"I'm serious. He's going to see if he can mentor Payton for his community service hours for graduation."

That shut them up.

"Okay, that's cool of him," Kelly said.

Natalie nodded. "Yeah, it is. But how did he find out about Payton?"

I hadn't told them about Asher living behind me or about listening to him play his guitar and sing outside my bedroom window. I hadn't told them about Asher giving me a ride or running into Payton skipping practice to hang out with his friends. And I hadn't said a word about talking to Asher last night.

So, I rectified the situation by telling them right then.

"Asher's your neighbor?" Kelly asked.

"You've been hanging out with him in your backyard," Natalie said.

"We've hung out twice."

"Why didn't you tell us?" Kelly asked.

I shrugged. "I don't know. There hasn't been anything to tell."

"Um, I'm pretty sure you just spent the last five minutes telling us a whole lot."

When she put it that way...

"Okay, when you put it all together, it seems like more than it is, but I promise nothing is going on."

Kelly leaned her shoulder into Natalie's and spoke out of the side of her mouth. "Do you think she's lying to herself or us?"

"Whatever," I said, turning my back on them, heading toward my first-period class. "You guys suck."

"See you at lunch?" Natalie called after me.

I waved over my shoulder. Their giggles followed me down the hall, making me smile. Natalie and Kelly were good friends. They always had my back and rarely let me off the hook.

Of course, the small ray of hope I'd been feeling about Payton, thanks to Asher, didn't eclipse the other source of anxiety that had nothing to do with my brother. Or the hot guy who had the voice of an angel.

As much as I tried to ignore his bad behavior, Leo Jessup just wouldn't let well enough alone. It occurred to me I'd been right. Pasting me into the walls on the ice translated into flirting in Leo's world because even after Asher laid into him at practice, Leo hadn't given up. Instead of messing with me on the ice, he did it at school.

Every time I turned around, he'd be right there, making stupid comments and leering. He'd managed to keep himself in check for the most part, but I dreaded each encounter. I'd become an expert at avoiding him.

Unfortunately, my desire to avoid Leo often conflicted with my unwanted desire to run into Asher. Like a junkie looking for her next hit, I'd been searching the halls between passing periods for any small glimpse of the boy I couldn't seem to get enough of.

"Hey, hey, Jordan."

Oh, no.

Distracted as I'd been with thoughts of Asher, I'd missed Leo walking up behind me.

He slung his arm around my shoulder, the aroma wafting to my nose from his armpit, making me gag a little.

"Get off me, Leo," I grunted, shoving his arm off my neck. I hadn't grown up with three brothers for nothing.

"Aw, come on, Jordan. You and me. What do you say?" He tried to put his arm around me a second time. I pushed him away again.

"In your dreams, Jessup. That's what I say." Was he crazy? What made him think I liked him like that? I didn't even like him not like that. Where were Natalie and Kelly when I needed them? But I knew where they were. On the whole other side of the school on their way to the cafeteria.

"Why you gotta be like that?" he whined, leaning over me, his hot breath disgusting on my cheek.

Had Leo always been so gross?

Then suddenly, from my other side, an entirely different sensation. A strong arm, heady scent, and sweet breath.

"Babe. I've been looking everywhere for you." Asher's arm settled around my waist, fusing our sides in a newly familiar way.

Babe?

"Wha-" I looked up into his gorgeous face to find him glaring at Leo.

Asher's gaze shifted until our eyes met. "I was looking for you," he said, his voice lowering to a timber I recognized from the hours I'd spent listening to him sing outside my bedroom window. Deep. Sultry.

My mouth went dry. "You were?"

"Yeah, I have something to tell you." His nose dipped toward my hair and I heard him inhale.

He'd caught me off guard. My knees felt weak. "Tell me?"

"Wait a second? What's going on here?" Leo asked the question I couldn't quite seem to form myself.

"Take a hike, man. Jordan's busy."

Was I?

Definitely.

"Busy doing what?" Leo asked, just as confused as me.

"Busy hanging out with me and not you. Now, go away." Asher's surprisingly hard stare had Leo backing up, his hands held up in surrender.

"Fine, man. Whatever." It didn't take him long to disappear into the crowd.

Asher and I watched until we couldn't see him any longer.

"What the heck, Jordan?" Asher asked in a tone that made my hackles rise. It felt like whiplash after being so affected by his nearness.

"What are you talking about?" I asked, still trying to shake off the haziness.

He snorted impatiently while herding me to the edge of the hall-way. As hockey players, we knew how to use our bodies to get people to move.

"Stop that." I might be used to getting pushed around, but that didn't mean I liked it.

"We talked about this. Why are you letting that guy bother you?" Asher towered over me, his body casting a shadow, giving the illusion of being secluded. "It's bad enough on the ice, but now he's doing it at school, too."

"He's just annoying." Not entirely true. I just didn't want Asher to think he had to fight my battles. He was already doing enough, helping with Payton.

Asher frowned. "It's more than that and you know it. Why haven't you told Joe? Or your dad? I can't believe neither of them has noticed."

The stuff on the ice wasn't that bad until you added in the school element. "I'm fine."

His dark eyes searched mine. I wanted to be mad at him for interfering, but I couldn't. What he'd done was kind of sweet.

"You called me *babe*." Did he see my pulse pounding in my throat? He stood so close, how could he not?

Asher's eyes darkened, his expression softening. "I had to get him away from you. I didn't know how else to do it without getting into a fight."

"Yeah, but now, he probably thinks we're, you know."

His lips turned up. The desire to reach out and touch them became almost impossible to resist. I didn't go gaga over boys. But something about Asher lured me in. Maybe his song. Or his willingness to help my brother. But what about my rule? Falling for Asher could be catastrophic.

Or it could be incredible.

Asher

"Yeah, but now, he probably thinks we're, you know," she said, her eyes widening.

Oh, yeah. I knew.

"And that would be a problem?" What could be the point of denying my attraction at this point? Jordan hit all my buttons in all the right ways. I noticed her. All. The. Time. That's how I saw Jessup messing with her. I couldn't keep my eyes off her.

After interfering at practice and getting my butt handed to me about it, I held back from saying anything, doing anything. But it was there. Every practice, I'd grit my teeth against the desire to paste that guy into the boards, but I understood. Jordan had something to prove. She didn't need me flying in to protect her. Hockey was a physical sport. Besides, her dad and her brother were both there every day, making me think I'd been overly sensitive because I wanted to kiss her.

Watching her shove Jessup's arm off her shoulder and then seeing him try to put it back, well, I couldn't take it anymore. I had to do something.

Now, Jessup was long gone. Jordan stood with her back against the wall in the now-empty hall, staring at me with those huge blue eyes of hers. Her pulse pounded in her neck, and I did something crazy.

With hands braced on either side of her head, I brushed my nose against the soft skin at the back of her jaw. Jordan looked tough, but she smelled like the most feminine thing I'd ever encountered.

"You smell so good," I murmured, inhaling deeply.

Her breath came out short and choppy. "I do?"

"Mhmm." I nodded, my nose brushing back and forth over her skin.

"What are you doing," she asked breathlessly.

"I don't want to be your enemy, Jordan." Stepping closer, I brought our bodies in contact with each other.

"You don't?"

"No."

"What do you want, then?"

I thought she'd never ask.

"I want to kiss you."

Her breath hitched. "You do?"

I nodded again. "Can I?"

She nodded.

Yes!

But first, we had to clear the air.

"Ms. Jackson said she'd talk to whoever's in charge at the middle school about Payton."

Jordan's hands gripped my sides. "She did? When?"

"I talked to her a few minutes ago. I was looking for you, though. I explained the situation to her. She thinks it's a great idea." Unable to wait any longer, I pressed my lips to her neck.

Jordan shivered, her fists clenching my t-shirt. "Asher–"

"I'm happy to help your brother if I can, but kissing you can't be about that." I lifted my head, needing to see her eyes. "I want to kiss you more than just about anything," I whispered. "But don't kiss me as a favor. Kiss me because you want to."

I drew my hands away from the wall and used them to frame her face. Her skin felt soft against my calloused fingertips, and with more patience than I knew I had, I waited.

"Jordan?"

"Oh, just do it already." Lifting onto her toes, Jordan brought her lips to mine.

It had been building, this need to hold her, kiss her. I couldn't hold back if I tried. My hands abandoned her cheeks to find her waist while our lips worked together, pulling, tugging, tasting.

I bent my knees and lifted her off the ground, gasping into her mouth. Her fingers threaded through my hair. My knees weakened.

Did that happen to guys?

I turned around and leaned my back against the wall. Jordan slid down my body, never breaking the seal of our lips. My arms and hands roamed over her back, into her hair. I'd never experienced such a passionate kiss.

One second, there, and the next, gone.

Chest heaving, she wiped her mouth with the back of her hand. Man, I wanted to pull her back and kiss her again.

"I should go."

"Jordan–" I said, but she stopped me.

"I'll talk to you later. I have to go."

I fell back against the wall and watched her leave. What the heck just happened? Did I kiss Jordan?

The tingling in my lips and the melody in my heart said yes.

What now?

Hell.

I had no idea, but I needed to play my guitar.

CHAPTER ELEVEN

Jordan

Holy smokes!

Did that just happen?

Did I just make out with Asher Sloane outside the cafeteria?

I needed some space.

No, I needed my friends.

Me: SOS

I ran into the restroom and waited for a reply. It didn't take long.

Hannah: What's up?

Alex: What's wrong?

Me: I did something stupid.

While I'd been hush-hush about Asher to Natalie and Kelly, I'd told Alex and Hannah everything. They didn't go to my school and wouldn't judge no matter what.

Alex: OMG! What?!?!

Hannah: Girl, what are you talking about?

I took a deep breath even though neither of them was around to appreciate my anxiety.

Me: I kinda, sorta, maybe kissed Asher.

I closed my eyes and waited for their reactions. It took long enough I imagined them staring at their phones in stunned silence.

And then my phone. Blew. Up.

Alex: You did WHAT?

Hannah: You go, girl! *kiss emoji*

Alex: What about Rule #1?

Hannah: Forget Rule #1. This guy must be HAWT *flames emoji*

Me: Looks aren't everything. But yes.

Hannah: I need pictures!

Alex: Jordan!

Hannah: Calm down, Alex. This isn't a bad thing. Jordan hasn't liked anyone. Ever.

Alex: Yes, I know, Hannah. But he's her teammate!

Hannah: So what? At least they're on the same team and not rivals.

Hannah: Wait. How did it happen? Where?

Me: Here at school. Just a few minutes ago. And I think I kissed him first.

Alex: What?!

Hannah: That's so awesome.

Me: No. It isn't awesome. Alex is right. He's my teammate. Kissing him was a mistake.

Neither of them responded for a full thirty seconds.

Hannah: Do you like him?

Did I like him? I hardly knew.

Why did I keep lying to myself? Maybe at first, I wanted to hate him, but he'd proven over and over I'd been too quick to judge. I allowed myself to get angry over petty things. I assumed he'd be shallow and self-centered because of his good looks. In reality, he'd defended me. Helped me. Been there for me when I needed someone to hold me while I cried. He didn't even complain when I soaked his t-shirt with tears and slobber.

Me: Yeah. *sigh*

Hannah: Then you should go for it!

Hannah: And no what if's!

She knew me too well.

Me: Alex?

Alex: I'm just going to say this. If you really like him, isn't it worth the risk?

Was Asher worth the risk?

I told my friends I'd talk to them later. I'd texted them in the middle of the school day. I had no idea how they'd gotten out of class or if they had lunch right now, too. But it made me laugh, imaging all three of us huddled in bathroom stalls in three different states. Those were the kind of friends I had, the kind who would lie about having to use the restroom to text a friend in need.

Somehow, I made it through the rest of the day. And without seeing Asher. I ran into Natalie and Kelly, but only in passing. After school, they both had to hurry to practice the same as me.

I dreaded running into Asher, knowing I needed more time to sort out my feelings, but he hadn't made it out to the parking lot by the time I drove away.

I took my time in the locker room getting ready. We had our first game in a week. I still had a lot to prove to my dad. Kevin Parks produced professional-quality athletes from his programs. Scouts came to see his teams play. And while I had no interest in playing for men's teams in the future, I hoped to catch the eye of some scout who could help me achieve my dreams.

Would spending time with Asher jeopardize all that? Or could the two aspects of my life remain separate? I meant what I said to my friends. I did like Asher. I liked the way I felt when I spent time with him. I loved the butterflies in my stomach when we flirted and how they took flight when we kissed.

Leo didn't bother me during practice. Neither did Asher. I appreciated him giving me space. However, I couldn't avoid him forever, nor did I want to. So when he waited for me at the edge of the ice after practice, I met him with a shy smile.

"Can I see you later? Outside?" he asked.

I nodded, then hurried to get out of there before I launched myself at him.

At home, Mom was up to her elbows in bows and asked me to put a casserole in the oven. I took a quick shower while it heated up and still had time to make a salad before Dad got home. He'd been taking Payton to school himself and picking him up from hockey practice.

"Where's your mom?" Dad asked, swiping a cucumber slice from the pile of chopped veggies I'd cut for the salad.

"Down in her workroom. She said she had a big order that has to be shipped tomorrow."

Dad nodded. "Thanks for making dinner. I'll go down and see how things are coming along." His footsteps thumped on the stairs down to the basement to Mom's craft room.

"So, what's going on with you and that guy?"

"Oh, my gosh! Payton, you scared me. I'm holding a knife."

Payton grinned and swiped a pepper.

Sometimes, I had to wonder why I loved my brother.

He pumped his eyebrows. "Is he your boyfriend?"

"No," I replied, my cheeks burning.

"Yeah, right. You want him to be. I can tell by how red your face is." He pointed a finger at my cheek. I batted it away.

"Shut up. You don't know anything."

Payton took a handful of baby carrots. "I know he's on your team," he said, tossing one in his mouth. "Do Dad and Joe know you're hanging out with him?"

"No. And why would they care? He's our neighbor. We go to school together." And we kissed earlier today, but who's keeping track? "We're just friends." Former enemies.

Payton popped another carrot into his mouth. "Uh-huh. Then how come I've seen you sneak into the backyard to hang out with him?"

"I wasn't sneaking, you little punk."

Payton just grinned. I opened my mouth to tell him just how off base he was when we heard Mom and Dad coming up the stairs.

I narrowed my eyes at my little brother, threatening him with a bit of non-verbal communication. He rolled his eyes and grabbed a plate.

For once, dinner didn't feel tense. I had no idea why, but I wouldn't complain. We were almost finished eating when Payton mentioned something that had my ears perking up.

"Hey, so I was going to talk to you guys about something that happened at school today," he said.

Both Mom and Dad froze, waiting to hear the bad news, but this time they didn't need to worry.

"What is it, Pay?" Mom asked.

"The school counselor called me down to her office and told me I'd been selected to be in this program to help some high schoolers get their service hours for graduation."

Dad frowned. "Doing what? I don't want you to miss hockey, Payton."

Dad's reticence worried me, but I knew Payton working with Asher wouldn't interfere with hockey at all, so I kept my mouth shut.

Payton rolled his eyes. "I won't have to miss anything, Dad. It's at school. Instead of going to art, I'll learn to play the guitar from one of the guys over at the high school. I brought home a permission form for you to sign since I'm switching my schedule to do it."

I could hardly contain my excitement. We'd only just talked about this last night. Already Asher had plans in motion. If he'd been beside me, I would have planted a big, fat kiss right on his lips.

"Play the guitar? Do you even want to learn the guitar?" Dad asked, still frowning, appearing confused.

"Dad, seriously. Who doesn't want to learn how to play the guitar?" And then, he stared straight at me when he said, "Chicks dig guys with guitars, don't they, Jord?"

Heat crept up my neck, but I shrugged, trying to keep it cool. "I don't know. I guess."

Payton smirked. I kicked him under the table, which only made him laugh.

"Well, I think it's wonderful," Mom said. "Do you know who it is? The high school student, I mean."

"Yeah, it's the new guy who lives behind us. Asher Sloane."

Dad's brows rose. "Asher? I didn't know he played the guitar."

"Me, either. But Jordan did."

Two sets of parental eyes swung to my side of the table. Payton grinned. My brother had a bit of the devil in him, I swear.

I cleared my throat. "I heard him playing the other day. In the backyard."

Dad's eyes narrowed as he connected the dots. He remembered me going into the backyard the other day, I knew it. It didn't matter. He wouldn't care. Now, he'd be watching, though.

Screw it. Might as well own it.

"As a matter of fact, I'm supposed to meet Asher right now, and since it's Pay's turn to do the dishes, can I be excused?" Take that, you little traitor!

Payton's lips thinned. He hated doing dishes.

Dad nodded, watching me closely. I avoided his gaze, but couldn't miss the smile on Mom's face. She keeps waiting for me to get a boyfriend. Not that Asher was my boyfriend! But me showing any interest in a guy made her happy. I'd be getting the third degree later.

I dumped my plate in the sink without even rinsing it off before I headed out the back door. I had no idea if Asher was even out there yet and I didn't care. I could wait because I had a big thank you to give to a certain teammate.

Asher

Jordan's body language after our kiss screamed *stay away*! It took all kinds of willpower, but I did it. Even at practice, when I could have found my way to her side, I held onto my pride a bit and focused on hockey.

Of course, I succumbed to my desires in the end when I asked her to meet me in the backyard. I was only human, after all.

I hadn't been able to stop thinking about that kiss. A melody began to play in my head, lyrics flowed, and after an hour in my bedroom picking, I'd written a song.

After dinner, I grabbed my guitar again and headed for the back door.

"Where are you going?" Dad asked from his recliner in the living room. "There's a game on."

I barely refrained from rolling my eyes. "Sorry, Dad. I'm gonna go hang out with Jordan."

"Who's Jordan?"

"A girl on my hockey team," I said before I could catch myself. Crap. I could have explained Jordan in so many other ways, why did I have to say that?

Dad's brows rose. "Really? I didn't know there was a girl on your team."

I shrugged. "It's not a big deal."

"No, just surprising. And she lives close by?"

"Yeah, in the house behind ours."

Dad frowned. "Isn't that Coach Parks's house?"

"Um, yeah. She's his daughter." I cringed, knowing how he'd interpret the information.

His face smoothed, confirming I'd been right. "Oh, I see."

"It's not like that. Jordan's good."

"I'm more worried about you. You ready for your first game next week?"

"Of course."

"Make sure you are. There's always someone watching." He faced the television again, while anxiety swirled in my gut.

I wanted to say I didn't care who watched, remind him I had no intention of playing hockey in college or anywhere else after high school, but that would just start an argument. Hopefully, I had better things to do. So, I let it go and went into the backyard.

The days were getting shorter. The sun had already set by the time I reached the trees at the back of our property. I hoped Jordan would be outside already and tried not to worry when I found our spot empty. Instead, I sat down on the hard seat and played the song I'd been working on earlier, humming along as I sang the words in my head. They weren't quite ready for anyone else to hear. Especially not Jordan.

I glanced up as I strummed the last chord.

"Hey, how long have you been there?"

"Just a couple of minutes." She smiled and sat down across from me.

I wanted to reach out and pull her down next to me, but I still held my guitar. I started to remove the strap from my shoulder, but she frowned.

"Aren't you going to keep playing?"

"You want me to keep playing?" I settled my guitar on my knee again and tried to hold back a smirk.

"Well, only if you want to." She bit her lip, drawing my attention to it.

A flash of heat coursed through my body. I knew what those lips felt like. Tasted like.

"Does this mean you like my music?"

She shrugged. "It's okay, I guess."

I shook my head and chuckled. "I'm never gonna catch a break with you, am I?"

"Probably not." She gestured toward my guitar. "Are you going to play something or not?"

"I'll play whatever you want," I told her, meaning it, too. She had no idea, but she had me wrapped around her pretty little finger.

"Play that song again. Is it new?"

I nodded. "I started it today. You like it?"

She grinned, not giving me an inch. "I can't believe you can just think up a tune and play it in a day."

"It doesn't always come so easy." My fingers moved over the guitar strings, but my eyes never left hers.

"Does it have lyrics?"

"Yeah, but they aren't ready yet." More like, I wasn't ready yet. I played for several minutes. Jordan leaned back in her chair and closed her eyes. Playing for an audience always made my blood pump. Playing for Jordan had it thrumming. I loved the serenity in her expression. I loved that my song had the power to make her stop and listen and ask me to keep playing.

Someday, I hoped I'd be playing in concerts with more than an audience of one, but for now, this was perfect.

Once I strummed the last chord, I held my hand over the strings to quiet them and watched as Jordan's eyes slowly opened.

"That one's okay."

I laughed out loud. "Thanks for keeping me humble."

She smiled. "No, thank you. Payton said they already had every-thing worked out for you two."

"It's not a big deal. Ms. Jackson acted right away to make it happen. I think she figured she'd better before I changed my mind or lost interest."

"You aren't going to do that, are you? Change your mind or lose interest?"

I reached across the distance between us to smooth the pucker between her eyes with my fingers. "No."

Her shoulders lost some of their starch. "Good. I think this could be good for him. He seemed excited when he told us about it at dinner."

"I'm glad. But Jordan, don't get your hopes up too high. Maybe Payton will get interested in music and straighten up, but maybe he won't." I hated the thought of letting her down. But in the end, Payton had to choose. I couldn't force him to change. He had to do that all on his own.

"I know." She stood up and paced the small patch of grass beside the furniture. "I do know. I'm just glad for something, anything, that might help him."

I rose to my feet and rested my guitar against the arm of the chair. "I hope it helps, too." However, we needed to talk about something else.

Reaching out, I took hold of Jordan's hips and pulled her close. Her mouth dropped open a little. Her hands rested against my chest.

"You let me kiss you earlier."

She nodded, a small smile tugging at her lips.

"If I remember right, you kissed me first."

"I can neither confirm nor deny," she said, making me laugh.

"You can't, huh? Well, can you confirm whether you're gonna kiss me again or not?"

"Hmm." She pretended to think about it. "I'm not sure. Maybe you should kiss me this time?"

I moved my hands from her hips to wrap my arms around her waist. "I think that can be arranged." I didn't hesitate this time, didn't tempt her to beat me to the punch. My lips collided with hers. I could have sworn I'd been kissing her forever. We fell into a tantalizing rhythm.

For several long moments, our mouths grew familiar, intimate. There were plenty of things I didn't know about Jordan Parks, but I knew she fit in my arms. I knew she tasted like my favorite flavor. I knew her hair felt soft against my skin. With that knowledge came a sense of possession. Jordan would always be her own person, but I certainly hoped some part of her could be mine.

"Jordan," I murmured between kisses. Darkness had fallen and we stood tucked beneath the trees. I didn't worry too much about getting caught making out with the Coach's daughter, but still.

"Hmm." Her arms wrapped tight around my neck and shoulders.

Forget it.

Never mind.

I'd take the risk.

CHAPTER TWELVE

Jordan

I woke up the next morning, my lips raw from kissing Asher the night before. Kissing? Could you call what happened between us something so simple as kissing? What did you call kissing for hours?

Making out?

I didn't like the sound of that, either. It had to be something more. We'd shared something more than hormonal teenagers getting their kicks. We'd connected. Kissing. Talking. Sharing.

Asher became someone more than the guy next door, or my teammate, or the idiot who stole my parking spot on the first day of school. He'd become my friend. Someone I could trust. For the first time, I wanted a boyfriend. Not just any boyfriend. Asher.

Asher offered to give me a ride to school, but I didn't want to invite any more questions than I'd already gotten the night. Mom and Payton had already gone to bed, but Dad still sat in his recliner, waiting up to lock the doors. I tried to keep my face in the shadows in case my lips were swollen from all that kissing, but he wasn't stupid.

When I arrived at school, Asher waited, leaning against the back of his car, looking like a model. I knew a moment of insecurity, because how could a guy like him like a tomboy like me, but then he saw me and his face split into a grin. Even I couldn't deny how happy he seemed.

"What do you think you're doing?" I asked after getting out of my car.

His face fell for a split second before smoothing out. He dropped his hands to his side and sauntered toward me.

"I'm not scared of you, Jordan Parks. Other guys at this school might be too chicken, but I'm not." To prove his point, Asher took me by my waist and pulled me into him.

"Too chicken to what?" I asked.

"To be your boyfriend."

My breath caught at the look in his eyes.

"What did you just say?"

"I like you, Jordan." He said it so simply, so honestly, I had to believe him.

"I like you, too." And I did. More than I wanted to admit. To him or myself. However, at this point, how could I deny it?

"Well, then?"

Could I do it? Throw caution to the wind and be Asher's girlfriend? Would this decision impact my dreams of playing hockey in the future? Or was it possible, as Hannah kept telling me, to separate Asher-potential-boyfriend from Asher-my-teammate?

"I have rules," I told him.

"Rules? What kind of rules?" He nuzzled my neck with his lips. All around us, people walked into school, but I didn't notice any of them. Just Asher.

"About dating teammates."

He paused in his sweet assault to look me in the eye but didn't say anything.

"I promised myself I wouldn't do that. Put the team at risk."

Asher shook his head. "It doesn't have to be like that."

"Yeah, but it could. We're already competing for the same position."

Asher growled. "So frustrating." His hands came up to frame my face. "I don't even care about hockey."

"Then explain it to me. Why are you even playing?" It made no sense.

His face twisted as he dealt with some internal debate. Finally, he exhaled a deep breath. "Because of my dad. He wants me to play."

"And you don't want to let him down?" I could understand the feeling.

He shook his head. "It's more than that. We made a deal. When I began to get serious about my music–" He looked up as though just realizing we still stood in the student parking lot and the bell would soon be ringing. "Can we talk about this later? We're going to be late."

"Are you kidding? You're just going to leave me hanging?" What did he hide?

He grinned. "No. I'm going to leave you with this." His lips crushed mine in an all-encompassing kiss that ended too soon.

Holy smokes!

"That's not fair," I said with my eyes still closed once he pulled away.

"Jordan," he said my name and waited for me to open my eyes.

"What?"

"I want this to work. I haven't felt–" He stopped again. This time I thought I might punch him.

"Haven't felt what?"

He dropped a quick kiss on my lips. "I haven't felt anything like this before. I don't want to give up. I want to give us a chance. Will you take a chance with me?"

Would I?

Right then, everything seemed scary. Being with Asher. Not being with him. Risking the balance that existed on our team.

But like him, I'd never felt anything like this, either. And letting it go hardly seemed an option.

"Yes. I'll take a chance with you."

Asher's mouth split into a beautiful, happy grin.

"But! But, we have to promise not to let our feelings mess with what's happening on the ice. Deal?" I held out my hand.

Asher took it but didn't shake it as I expected. Instead, he held it securely as he leaned down to kiss me again. "Deal."

We walked into school hand in hand. I'd never once held hands with a guy at school before, and it seemed everyone noticed me holding Asher's. Part of me wanted to rip my hand out of his grasp and push him away, but why? I didn't feel ashamed of him, just the opposite.

Asher squeezed my hand just as Natalie came barreling around the corner, giving me just the warning I needed to brace for impact.

Natalie's eyes widened and her mouth dropped open when she saw us together. Then almost immediately, her expression turned smug.

"Whatever is about to happen, I am so sorry," I said just loud enough for him to hear.

Asher laughed as he took hold of my shoulders, pushing me in front of him like a shield.

"Chicken!"

"You know it." His breath hit the skin on my neck gave me goose-bumps. He must have noticed because he blew gently again and chuckled.

"Not funny."

"It's a little funny."

Ten feet in front of us, Natalie squealed, drawing the attention of anyone in a fifty-mile radius. "OMG! Did I call it or what?"

"Nat, calm down." I should just permanently stain my cheeks red. It would be simpler. I wanted to switch places and hide behind Asher.

"No way! You two are just too cute together. I'm so excited for you." She punctuated her statement with another squee and a hug that sandwiched me between her and Asher.

"What on earth is going on?" Kelly asked, watching us with one hand on her hip.

Before I could answer, Natalie broke away to hug Kelly. "Jordan and Asher are together."

Kelly glanced at Asher and me, where we were indeed standing together. "Um, yeah. So?"

"Are they always like this?" Asher whispered in my ear.

"I told you," I said out the side of my mouth.

Natalie rolled her eyes as she exhaled an impatient breath. "No. Together, together."

Kelly's brows rose. "Oh." She took a second look at us, noticing Asher's hand on my hip and the way his chin rested on my shoulder. "Oh!"

"Yeah." Natalie nodded with satisfaction.

Enough embarrassment for one morning, thank you!

"Okay, guys. Let's move along. We're drawing a crowd," I said, waving my friends forward. And it was true. Several people had stopped to gawk at Asher and me.

It would be hard to miss all the looks he got from girls at school on a regular day. But today? Holding my hand? Now, they were staring at me. And not in a friendly way. I'd be lucky if I didn't get my eyes clawed out by day's end.

"Does this mean you're going to sit with us at lunch, Asher?" Natalie asked.

"Oh, um–" he looked at me. "We haven't discussed it, but I usually hang out with Jarom and the guys during lunch. With passing periods on either side, we can usually jam for almost an hour."

"Jam?" Kelly asked.

"Yeah, I kind of joined their band. We practice during lunch since I don't have much time after school." He shot me a look. "With hockey and everything."

I got a warm feeling knowing everything referred to hanging out with me.

"That is so cool," Natalie said.

"Don't be such a groupie, Nat." Kelly rolled her eyes.

Natalie's cheeks flushed. "I'm not a groupie," she said to Kelly before turning back to Asher and me. "Although, I would love to hear you guys play sometime."

Asher nodded. "I'm sure that could be arranged. Let me talk to the guys." He glanced down at his empty hand and stopped. "Dang. I left my guitar in my car. I better go get it before the bell rings." He turned to me, his warm brown eyes melting my heart a little. He was so very hot. "See you later?"

"Yeah."

"Good." He kissed me quickly before smiling at my friends and hurrying back the way we came.

Natalie and Kelly flanked me, one on either side, as we watched him go.

"I can't believe you get to kiss him." A comment I might have expected from Natalie, but it came from Kelly.

"You better watch your back, Jordan. Every girl in this school's crushing on your new boyfriend."

I cringed, knowing she was right. "We better get to class."

"He must be pretty good if Jarom asked him to be in their band. I've heard them a few times. They're not bad," Kelly said.

"Really? I didn't know that. When did you hear them?" I asked.

Kelly shrugged. "At the concert in the park thing they do over the summer. I went with Angie. Jarom, I can't remember what their band is called, but Bash and Adam are good, too."

"Well, Asher's amazing." My friends knew all about me listening to Asher out my bedroom window by now. "And guess what else?" I told them about Asher mentoring Payton, teaching him to play the guitar and sing.

"Wow, that's awesome," Kelly said.

We'd stopped outside my first-period class. They both had classes close by and the bell would ring any second.

"It will be if it helps keep him out of trouble."

Asher

A week later, I still couldn't believe Jordan agreed to be my girlfriend. And even though we tried to keep things on the down-low, especially at hockey, I couldn't deny how crazy I felt about her.

Her brother, Payton, on the other hand, was a whole different story. I wasn't crazy about him at all.

"Dude, why are you even doing this?" I asked him after our third day working together. I hadn't told Jordan what a little turd her brother could be, but that's precisely the word I would use to describe him. She probably knew, anyway.

Payton slumped down in his seat, one of the school's guitars held haphazardly in his grip. The kid had no respect. "What do you care? Let's just do the time, man. It's not like anyone's checking on us or anything."

Bingo.

Everyone had something to motivate them. I had no idea what motivated Payton, but with one little sentence, he revealed it to me.

"Oh, really? Is that what you think?"

Payton frowned, his eyes meeting mine for the first time since I walked into the middle school band room. "What do you mean?"

"Do you think Ms. Jackson and Mr. Hooper are going to just let us mess around in here for an hour every day without any kind of accountability?" I made a scoffing noise. "You're crazy." I sat back in my chair with my arms crossed over my chest and waited.

Payton sat forward. I tried not to cringe at the careless way he handled the instrument in his hands. "What are you talking about? No one said anything to me. What do I have to do, take a test or something?"

That would have been easier to plan than what I had in mind, but the stakes weren't high enough. If Payton had an ounce of his sister's competitiveness, a test wouldn't cut it.

"A test? Dude, no." I shook my head and sighed. "Man, you have to perform. In front of the whole school." I hoped I wasn't lying to him. As soon as I finished with Payton, I'd have to pay a little visit to Mr. Hooper. And then I'd have to convince Jordan to help me pull this off.

Payton's face turned pale. "I have to what?"

"Yeah, there's gonna be a school talent show and you have to perform. That's part of the program. They don't want us to just sit in here and do nothing. And to prove we haven't been-" I clapped my hand down on his shoulder. "You have to perform what you've learned."

"No. No. I'm not doing it." Payton shook his head, looking dazed.

"Oh, really? Then I guess you'd rather do the other thing?" I was taking a chance and I knew it, but what other choice did I have?

Payton's eyes narrowed. "What do you know about that?"

Ha! I didn't know anything, but I was right. Working with me had been option number two, the lesser of two evils. Payton had been a bad boy, indeed.

I shrugged. "Does it matter?" His eyes wavered with a flicker of doubt. "What's it going to be, Payton?"

He still wanted to be the tough guy, the one with the upper hand. "Maybe I don't care. Maybe I just did this because it sounded easier." He looked me in the eye. "Performing in a talent show doesn't sound easy."

I'd have to sweeten the pot. An idea had occurred to me as we talked. Probably overkill, but I didn't care. No skin off my nose either way.

"Okay, Payton. Fine. I'm willing to make you a deal because you're my girlfriend's little brother. Consider it a friends and family thing."

Payton's top lip curled. "I can't believe you kiss my sister."

"Believe it. And I love every second of it." I held back a laugh while he pretended to throw up in his mouth.

"You ready to hear my offer?" I asked.

Payton hesitated, but only for a second, before nodding. Whatever the other option might be, it must suck.

"Okay, if you go through with this and you don't give me any crap while we work to get you ready to perform a song in front of all your friends-" Was it my imagination, or did he turn a little green? "If you commit to this, right here, right now, there's a ticket in it for you."

"A ticket? For what?" I'd piqued his interest. Good. Now for the clincher.

"A ticket to see Carly Ryan in concert on November first."

Payton's mouth dropped open before he caught himself and laughed. "Yeah, right, man. Like you have a ticket to see Carly Ryan."

"Not just one ticket, three. One for you. One for me. And one for Jordan." Or I would as soon as I made a phone call. It would only be a matter of one ticket, however, because two would already be waiting for me at will call the night of the concert, just like they always were and had been since she hit it big when I was five. It didn't matter where she was in the world, I'd get a text before every show letting me know she'd left two tickets with my name on them at will call. I'd taken her up on them a few times, and only since I got my driver's license, but they were always there.

Payton scoffed. "How do you have three tickets to see Carly Ryan? Those tickets sold out weeks ago."

The whole tour had sold out in under an hour.

"What'll it be, Payton? This is the deal. Take it or leave it, but I'm only going to offer it once. I don't have to sit here and torture myself every day. I can do something else to get my hours." I acted as though I didn't care, but I did. Jordan would be heartbroken if this didn't work out.

"You seriously have Carly Ryan tickets and you'll give one to me if I do a stupid talent show?"

I nodded. "I seriously do. And I will. But this isn't a joke. You have to work hard and do a good job. You can't just go up there and play Chopsticks, so to speak, and think we have a deal."

Payton chewed his lip. I could almost see the wheels turning in his head. "Carbine is opening for Carly Ryan. They're my favorite band."

And just like that, folks, I had him. "Dude, are you kidding? Because I can introduce you to them."

"Holy sh— I mean, crap! Are you serious? But how?" Payton eyed me with suspicion. "You can get tickets to a sold-out concert and introduce me to the opening act? How is that possible?"

Well, crap. I didn't want to answer all that just yet. "I have my ways, don't you worry. And Payton." I paused, waiting for him to meet my gaze. "For now, this is between you and me. You can't run around telling everyone. Not even Jordan." I gave him a hard stare, hoping he'd realize I was serious. "That's a deal-breaker, kid. Got it?"

"Dude, if you can get me in to meet Carbine, I'll do whatever you want."

I held out my hand. "All I want is for you to come in here and learn a song for the talent show. Deal?"

Payton held out his hand. "Deal."

"Alright, man. I'll see you next week."

Payton shook his head. "No, man. I'll see you tonight. First game. Remember?"

Oh, yeah.

Crap.

CHAPTER THIRTEEN

Jordan

I'd never had a boyfriend before. Holding hands at school, waiting for each other during passing periods, feeling that sweet little flutter in my stomach whenever he smiled that smile, the one meant just for me—I liked it.

I'd begun to think all my worries about dating a teammate were foolish. We went to school, to practice, made out in his backyard. Hockey didn't become an issue. Even my dad and brother seemed pretty chill about everything. Joe teased me relentlessly, making kissy faces whenever I skated past him during practice, but what did I expect? As far as Dad, he limited his concerns to flipping the back porch light on and off when he felt Asher and I had been secluded in the darkness too long.

Even Leo had let up a bit.

Tonight, however, we had our first hockey game. Asher offered to give me a ride to the rink, but I declined. I knew myself. If tonight ended with disappointment, I wouldn't be any fun to be around after the game. A part of me needed the separation from him in case things didn't go how I wanted them to.

Several members of the team clustered around Dad's office two hours before the game started. On his door, a single sheet of white paper had been taped. The sheet listed who would be in the starting lineup that night.

Asher hadn't arrived yet.

I walked down the hall toward the door, and that sheet, by myself, my heart pounding. I wanted that starting spot so badly I could taste it. Asher and I avoided conversations about the team other than to complain about drills and sore muscles to each other.

My brother Joe stepped out of the middle of the huddle of players. He didn't see me at first, but when he did, his expression went from steely determination to wariness.

Asher would start.

I stopped in the middle of the hall. Joe approached me. He knew I wouldn't want his pity, but I gratefully accepted his support when he ruffled my hair as he walked by on his way to the locker room.

Hockey was a team sport. Dad made the best decision for the team. I got it, I did. But it still hurt.

I dressed for the game in the women's locker room. Loud metal-head music echoed from the men's locker room down the hall along with the deep intonations of my teammates as they razzed each other and got pumped up for the game.

I told myself to buck up. I wanted this, that meant digging deep. Even playing off the bench, my team needed me. I couldn't let them down.

Dad made sure all the guys were dressed adequately before calling me into the locker room for a pre-game pep talk. Asher sat in the front with all the other starters, easily the best looking guy in the room. I still thought him too pretty to be a hockey player. His eyes caught mine. I forced a smile. He didn't need to be worried about my feelings at a time like this.

We had a game to win.

. . .

And we did win. I went in a few times to give Asher a breather, but for the most part, he'd been the guy. To say I'd been humbled would be an understatement. My butt dragged out of the locker room to find Asher waiting.

"Hey." He took a step toward me, then stopped, his eyes worried.

"Hi. Good game."

"I, um-"

"Jordan," my dad's voice interrupted. We both turned to find him standing in the doorway to his office. "I need to talk to you for a minute." He glanced at Asher. "Now."

Dad disappeared back into his office.

Asher frowned. "What's that about?" I could tell a part of him didn't want to let me go. Sweet. He needed some reassurance.

Rising onto my toes, I kissed his cheek.

He sighed, all visible tension draining from his body. "Can I wait for you?"

"I'd be mad if you didn't."

One side of his mouth curled into a crooked smile. "Can't have that, now can we?"

I walked back toward Dad's office. "I'll be right back."

"I'll be right here."

Dad sat on the edge of his desk. "Come in and shut the door."

I did as he asked.

"I wanted to talk to you here rather than waiting until we got home because what I'm about to say comes from your coach and not from your dad."

I gulped. "Okay."

"Jordan, I'm proud of you."

Excuse me, what?

"Um." I didn't know what to say.

"It's not easy playing the bench. It's something you're not used to, but you did your job and played every minute with all you had. I appreciate your effort. You work hard, you're an asset to our team, and I'm glad you're here." He paused to smile. "That last part might have been more dad than coach."

I rolled my eyes, fighting a grin. "Sixty-forty?"

He laughed. "More like eighty-twenty." He pushed off his desk to hug me.

"Thanks, Dad."

"You're welcome. Now, go celebrate with your teammates. I think Joe said everyone was headed over to the diner."

"I'll see what Asher wants to do."

Dad glanced at the door. "He's a good kid. Go easy on him, okay?"

"Who me?"

"Yeah, you. You forget, I know you." Dad grabbed his jacket off a hook on the wall. I opened the door for both of us to find Asher standing right where I'd left him.

Dad pumped his eyebrows at me. "Have her home by midnight," he said in his best dad voice.

"Yes, sir." Asher nodded. He pushed away from the wall and reached for my hand. "Ready?"

I nodded. "See you later, Dad."

We didn't waste any time exiting the rink. Most of the team had already left and only a few straggling spectators remained. Asher led me to his car, parked in the middle of the lot by itself. When we reached the passenger's side, instead of opening the door, he spun me around, his lips meeting mine.

"You have no idea how much I've been sweating it since I saw that list," he said against my lips.

Gripping the front of his shirt, I brought him closer. His mouth moved across mine. I loved kissing him.

"I'm not mad at you," I said between kisses. "I have no right to be."

Asher pulled back to look at me. "If it wasn't for me, you'd have started tonight."

I shook my head. "No, if I played better than you, I would have started tonight. But I didn't. I don't. It's not your fault you're a better hockey player, Asher. It's mine. If I want to play at the next level, then I have to play at the next level. And I'm not there yet. That's on me."

He leaned back against the car, his hands on my hips, dragging me with him. I thought he might kiss me again, but he didn't. Instead, he held me. With our bodies pressed together and my head on his chest, I felt an emotion I'd never experienced before. A closeness. A connection. Asher was beginning to mean something to me. Maybe that explained why I didn't hate him for being better than me, because fair or not, if it had been anyone else, I would have hated their guts.

"Maybe I could help you," he said. "We could work out after practice instead of making out in the backyard."

I put my hand over his mouth. "Don't talk like that." His eyes sparkled. "Making out with you is my favorite time of day."

Huh.

Could it be true?

Hockey practice had always been my favorite time of day.

Had Asher replaced hockey in my heart? No. I didn't believe it, not after such a short amount of time. But then, I remembered the words my dad had spoken a few weeks ago when he reminded me to live my life and not everything revolved around hockey. I didn't believe him when he said it, but now, I wondered if he might be right.

Asher pulled my hand away from his mouth. "Well, then we would never want to stop doing that, but how about we stay for an extra thirty minutes or so? My dad would be thrilled. And I don't think yours would care, either."

I knew mine wouldn't. And it could be a lot of fun.

"We could do other stuff, too. Like weight training or speed training. My dad got me into speed training a few years ago. It's changed my game more than anything else."

Tipping my head back, I kissed his chin. "You'll share your secrets with me?"

Asher groaned. "Babe, I'll share all my secrets with you," he said before kissing me gently.

"Really? All of them? Because I seem to remember a certain explanation you were going to give about the real reason you play hockey." I lifted one brow.

He dropped his forehead down to meet mine. "I thought you forgot about that."

"You mean, you hoped I did."

Asher sighed. "Okay. You're right. I owe you. But it's not as big a deal as you might think."

"Then it won't be a big deal to tell me."

"Not here. Let's go somewhere else."

Asher

"Are you hungry?" I asked once we'd settled into my car.

"Starving. Aren't you?"

"Yeah. Did you want to meet everyone at the diner?"

Jordan gave me a look.

"I'm not stalling. I promise. Just trying to be polite and ask what you want."

"I want to drive through somewhere and then go sit in the park to eat. And talk."

A woman who knew her mind. I liked it.

"Okay. Where do you want to get food?"

"Not where the team is, somewhere else. I know. Turn left at the next light." Jordan gave me directions to a fast food joint on the opposite side of town from the diner where the rest of our teammates celebrated our first win. We should have joined them, but I didn't care too much and I had a feeling Jordan didn't either.

We ordered our food. Once we had it, Jordan directed me to a park on the edge of town. I realized I'd been there before with Shari and Caleb when we first moved here.

I carried our shakes while Jordan grabbed the paper bag with our burgers and fries.

"This okay?" I asked, pointing to a wooden picnic table.

"Perfect."

For the next few minutes, we ate and talked about the game. We were both hungry. Soon all we had left were our shakes.

"How is it you didn't leave a girlfriend back in Minnesota?"

"I don't know. I've had girlfriends, but not anyone I cared about beyond a few dates." Besides, everyone in Minnesota knew everything about me. Not always a good thing.

Jordan bumped my shoulder with hers. "I bet you left a string of broken hearts behind."

"Maybe. But I doubt it." Why were we talking about this? "What about you? Jarom says he's never seen you with anyone before."

Even in the dim light from distant street lights, Jordan's cheeks lit. "I don't know. I guess I never met anyone I wanted to spend time with."

"Until you met me." I puffed out my chest.

Jordan laughed. "Yeah, you've ruined me for anyone else."

I liked the sound of that. "Come here." The night had grown colder. I moved back on the picnic tabletop and threw one leg behind Jordan so I could bring her closer. She nestled into my chest.

"Seriously, though. You never liked anyone?" I had no idea why I pursued this line of questioning, but I kind of wanted to understand why she picked me.

"Not really. I've been focused on hockey. My brothers are a little protective." She looked up at me. "Although, Joe seems to like you. Payton hasn't said anything bad, either, so it looks like I made the right choice waiting around for you."

"I'm flattered." Truth.

She tugged on my shirt front. "Tell me. Why don't you want to play hockey? And why do you do it if you don't love it? And for real, how did you get so good? It takes so much motivation to work so hard."

"I made a deal with the devil," I told her, only half kidding.

Jordan shifted in my arms to see me better. "What do you mean?"

Where to start?

"My dad played hockey in college. He wanted to play in the NHL but he and my mom were in a car accident. She was pregnant with me and the accident made her go into labor early. Just a couple of weeks, but I had to stay in the hospital for a week. Dad's knee got destroyed in the accident. He was in surgery when I was born. The accident changed things. Dad couldn't play hockey anymore. Mom had postpartum depression... On top of that, they had a lot of medical bills."

"Wow. That must have been hard." Jordan's hand traced the line of my jaw, her face etched with concern.

"I don't remember anything from back then, but we're all still dealing with the aftermath." I caught her hand in mine and pressed my lips to her palm. I'd never really talked to anyone about this stuff except Shari. After she'd been married to my dad for a while, we started talking about things I'd never been able to discuss with my dad. She helped us in the ways we needed.

"So, what happened?" Jordan asked.

"Dad got better, but Mom didn't. She didn't get help for her depression. When she turned to music as a sort of therapy, my dad got upset, accused her of ignoring me, ignoring him, she couldn't take it anymore. When I was two, she packed a suitcase and her guitar and took off in the middle of the night. We never heard from her again until I was five." When my dad saw her on the cover of a country music magazine in the grocery store checkout line. He immediately tracked her down and filed for divorce.

Jordan frowned. "Do you see her much?"

I shook my head. "I've seen her a handful of times. She sends me text messages and a check in the mail for my birthday and every major holiday. Even some of the obscure ones like National Rubber Duckie Day."

"Does that even exist?"

"January thirteenth."

She giggled. "That's funny."

I agreed.

"I don't understand what all that has to do with hockey, though."

"Well," I sighed. "Part of the reason my mom left had to do with her music. Dad thought all the time she spent singing and playing guitar was a waste. She'd do that rather than take care of me or the house while he worked. He never told me, but my step-mom did after they'd been married for a while that Dad would come home from work. I'd be naked except for a dirty diaper, screaming for food while my mom locked herself in a room with her guitar."

"Oh, that's awful."

"Yeah, I'm okay with not remembering any of it." I picked up my melty shake and took a sip. "She left us to pursue her dream of playing music professionally. It was her dream, not us. That's all there is to it.

Dad has never forgiven her. He blames music for ruining their marriage, for the way she didn't take care of me the way she should have, for everything. I have pictures of me sitting on her lap. She's playing the guitar, and I'm trying to play, too. Dad tried to keep me away from it, but after she left I was inconsolable, carrying around a toy guitar, not one with strings, but one that had buttons that would light up when you pressed them. Shari told me Dad would hide it and I'd cry. He finally gave in and bought a seventy-five dollar guitar from the toy section."

"So, he wants you to play hockey because he doesn't want you to become focused on music like your mom did?"

"It sounds crazy, but he's convinced if I'm good enough at hockey to play professionally, I'll develop a passion for it. And it's not like I don't enjoy hockey, I do." I gave her a lopsided grin. "And I probably do like it more because I'm good at it, but I can't deny the music inside me. It's there. I can't stop it, and I don't want to. He just doesn't understand. For him, music is something that brought him a lot of pain. He blames Mom's choices on music, but really, she's just selfish. It has nothing to do with music. Lots of people have careers doing what they love and still make time for their families."

Jordan's hand caressed my forearm. "And you made a deal with the devil."

I nodded. "When I was younger, he'd take my guitar away from me as punishment. Now, it's more play hockey, keep up my grades, and he keeps his grumbling to a minimum. But I have to excel, work for it. Hockey can't just be a hobby, I have to treat it like a goal."

"Music is your motivation. Even in hockey."

I breathed a small sigh of relief. She got it. She understood. A weight lifted off my shoulders.

"I don't want to bag on your dad or anything, but that's kind of unfair. I mean, you aren't your mom."

"How could I be, knowing what she did to us?" I shook my head. "I've talked to Shari about it. My mom was sick. She had untreated depression. That's part of the reason she left us. And I think Dad knows, he just still struggles with his own issues. I wish he'd go to counseling. He has a lot of pent-up anger at my mom he needs to deal with. But he won't." I turned to Jordan. "I don't want to be like either of them."

"I think that means you won't be."

We sat silent for a few moments. I enjoyed being with Jordan. I felt closer to her than anyone. I knew she had no idea how much it meant to me to be able to share my past with her and for her to accept me for me.

"So, what happened to your mom? Did she ever make it with her music?"

CHAPTER FOURTEEN

Jordan

I didn't get a straight answer to my question about Asher's mom. He'd already revealed more than he probably wanted about his family drama, so I let it go. If he wanted me to know more, he'd tell me. That didn't mean I wasn't tempted to Google famous people with the last name Sloane, but I held myself back. She likely didn't use that name anyway.

The night in the park changed things between us. I understood Asher better. Understanding brought compassion. And a fierce protectiveness. I knew Asher loved his dad and respected him, but I wanted to scream at him for creating this conflict in his son.

Of course, I couldn't do that.

Over the next few weeks, life settled into a pattern. Asher began picking me up in the mornings. It gave us another ten minutes to be together, and we were at the point in our relationship where every moment counted. I asked him to not park in my spot. Eventually, it filled each day with a different car. I'd been holding onto something trivial and decided to fill the void in my life from my brothers moving out by reaching out more through phone calls and group texts. It's made a difference.

Some days, I'd sit with Natalie and Kelly during lunch, but others I followed Asher to the practice room and listened to him and the other guys practice. They were good, and I liked hanging out with Jarom, Adam, and Bash. It took a while to get them to loosen up around me, but I liked to think we were becoming friends. I even helped them come up with a new band name. The original name before Asher came along had been Three Fold, but since they added a fourth member, that name didn't make sense anymore. They'd been throwing names around while I just listened, skirting around a theme but not quite finding the right name. Finally, it came to me. When I blurted it out, they'd all stopped to stare before each head nodded. That's how they became *Breakout*.

After school each day, we had practice, and after practice, Asher insisted we work for thirty minutes on speed training. He taught me how to use exercise bands to build explosive power. I couldn't believe the difference it made on the ice.

"Hey, babe?" Asher rolled over to face me. We were lying side by side on the grass, completely spent after our workout.

"Yeah." My muscles ached. I didn't want to move for the next week. Maybe someone would bring me a blanket, and I could sleep right there.

"I need to tell you something."

Oh, that didn't sound good. I rolled onto my side, so we faced each other. "What?"

For a split second, I panicked. What if he wanted to tell me he didn't like me anymore? Or he wanted to take a break or something? We'd been spending a ton of time together. I didn't mind, but what if he'd grown tired of me?

Then, he reached out, a tiny smile lighting his face as he brushed his fingertips down my cheek. "How can you still be so pretty after the workout we just did?"

"Stop it." I batted his hand away, but couldn't hold back my grin.

He laughed. "Okay, here goes. Jarom got us a gig."

My eyes widened. "Really? Where?"

"It's nothing big. But there's this thing they do in the park once a month."

I nodded because I knew about those. Natalie had kissed Finn at one over the summer. I didn't get into indie bands very much, so they weren't my thing, but I knew people did.

"Jarom said they've done a few shows in the park and the organizers invited them back. There's not any money in it or anything, just exposure, but we want to do some of my songs."

"That's cool. When is it?"

"Next week. On Saturday. It'll be after our game, and I wondered if you would want to go." He seemed nervous to ask, and I wondered why.

"Of course, I want to go. Why would you think otherwise?" I searched his face for clues to what he was thinking or feeling.

"I don't know," he said.

I noticed his cheeks were red again after they'd already cooled from the exertion of exercising. Was he embarrassed?

"Why are you shy about this?" I asked.

He rose onto his elbow and rested his head in his hand. I mirrored his position. He set his other hand on my waist. "I'm not. I'm excited about it."

I got this weird feeling that made me kind of sick. "Do you not want me to go, and you're just asking because you feel like you have to?"

Asher frowned. "What? No. Why would you ask me that?"

"Because you're acting like a weirdo." Pushing off the ground, I sat up.

He scrambled to sit up, too. "I'm not trying to be." Asher shook his head and raked both hands through his hair. "I have no idea what's happening here." He reached for my hands and held them tight as he stared directly into my eyes. "Jordan, I have a gig in the park next Saturday, and more than anything, I want my girlfriend there to support me. Will you please, please go?"

I studied his expression for any sign he didn't mean what he said. I couldn't find one, but I still felt unsettled.

"Of course I'll go."

Asher exhaled a deep breath and threw his arms around me. "Thank you. I'm sorry," he said into my neck. "Whatever that was, I'm sorry."

I wanted to feel reassured, but part of me kept waiting for the other shoe to drop. Everything had been so amazing, so easy. We felt perfect for each other, almost too good to be true. I didn't want to go looking for trouble, but I admit to being on the lookout. He'd become important. Every day I got to know him more. Every day he became more tightly woven into the pattern of my life, and I worried about what would happen if he wanted to pull away. Would everything unravel? Would I be able to stitch it all back together?

I hoped I never found out.

Asher

How, in such a short time, did I get so involved? School. Hockey. The band. Mentoring Payton. Not to mention choir and jazz band.

And Jordan.

Especially Jordan.

It's like my life in Minnesota never existed. I hadn't looked back once. I realized my friends back there didn't see me for me. They saw me as someone. Carly Ryan's son. It had been impossible to hide my identity. Everyone knew, had always known, and they asked questions.

Can you get me tickets to your mom's next show?

Are you gonna be a singer just like her, Asher?

Do you think you're better than everybody?

What's it like having a mom who never comes to see you?

None of them had any idea what they were talking about. I'd come to terms with Carly Ryan. She didn't want to be Carly Sloane, wife and mother. Maybe I wished she'd have figured herself out before she had me, but then, I wouldn't be here. I guess, if anything, I owed her for giving birth to me, and maybe that was enough.

Jordan had had so many opportunities to ask me about my mom, but she hadn't. One day I'd tell her how much that meant to me. Until then, I'd just be thankful.

"Dude, show me that part again," Payton demanded. He'd come a long way in the month we'd been working together and not just musically. I liked to think we'd bonded, and he did look up to me as a mentor. Not that I presented the best example, but better than most.

"Like this." I played the notes again, almost exaggerating my movements so he could see.

We'd learned to compensate for having opposite dominant hands. I showed him how to play left-handed while he had to figure out how to adjust and play right-handed, but it worked because ultimately, the mechanics were the same. I'd also shown him some online videos he could watch, and I could tell he had.

We decided to do a song he already knew well by his favorite band. Carbine was a bit country, a bit blues, and lot rock. It helped I liked them, too, and already knew a lot of their songs.

We only had two and a half weeks left until the talent show and call me crazy, but I knew Payton would be ready.

We worked on the song for a few more minutes, but then Payton stopped playing.

"Hey, Asher?"

"Yeah?" I started picking out a tune I'd been humming all morning.

"Can I ask you a question?"

Something about the tone of his voice made me stop and look at him. "Sure, kid. Anything."

Payton hadn't opened up much, but we talked a little. Ms. Jackson gave me some guidelines. I could be Payton's friend, but I wasn't a trained professional. I couldn't be his counselor.

"What would you do if-" he stopped, his face twisting with indecision.

I stared at him for a second. "Is this a question for you or a friend?"

His face cleared a little. "A friend."

I nodded. "Okay. What is it?"

"Let's say this friend-" he gave me a look— "Payson has another friend, named Toby. And Toby gets in trouble a lot."

I raised my eyebrows. Payton had the good grace to appear somewhat remorseful.

"No, man. Like real trouble."

"Okay. What about this Toby guy?" It made sense Payton had friends who got into real trouble as he put it.

"Well, Payson and Toby have been friends for a long time. But Toby's bad news and Payson's trying to..." Payton glanced at the ground and shrugged before meeting my eyes again. "Payson wants to stop doing that stuff with Toby."

Hmm. I sat back in my chair and studied Payton. "What's keeping Payson from telling Toby to take a hike?"

Payton made a face. "We've, um, *they've* been friends a long time. Payson's kind of hoping Toby will, you know, stop doing all the other stuff."

"Toby's the reason Payson's been getting in so much trouble?" I asked, lifting one brow to let Payton know I knew exactly who we were talking about.

Payton's shoulders fell, but he kept up the pretense. "Yeah, man. It's like he's two different people. When he's around Toby, he wants Toby to still like him, so he does sh-, I mean, crap he shouldn't." Payton smiled, guilty as hell. "Sometimes, it's kind of fun, right. But then," his smile died. "But then, he gets home, his parents are mad, and his mom's crying and he knows he's just a punk kid who's all messed up."

Well, crap.

Now what?

I took a full minute without saying anything to think about what Payton had just told me. I knew exactly how he felt. I'd been there myself, done stupid stuff because I wanted my friends to keep being my friends, and felt like I had to follow along for that to happen.

Sitting forward in my chair, I rested my elbows on my knees. "Dude, you already know the answer, right? You can't let other people decide your destiny. This guy, Toby, he doesn't care about you." Payton frowned, and I didn't know if it was because I'd hit a nerve or because I'd dropped the Payson lie. Or both. "I know it sounds cliche, but it's true. If Toby was your friend, he wouldn't pressure you to do things you don't want to do. Man, five minutes of fun is not worth a lifetime of negative consequences. I promise."

Payton chewed on his lip. "I told him I joined a band the last time he wanted to hang out. He made fun of me. Said my band probably sucked. It's not even true. I just needed an excuse other than hockey because he knows I've skipped practice to hang out with him before. That's why my dad takes me, but Toby thinks I can ditch my dad, no big deal."

"Payton, that's manipulation. He's playing on your emotions to get you to do what he wants you to do. Don't fall for that bull. And if he was your friend, he wouldn't want you to get in trouble with your dad." I thought for a minute. "Why don't you start a band? Do you know anybody who plays?" Payton had a decent singing voice.

Payton nodded. "That's kind of why I said it. I've been talking to some guys. We all like Carbine, and I told them about working with you." His eyes lit for the first time since we started talking. "We were saying how cool it would be to start playing together."

"Dude, that's your answer." I hoped he could see it as plain as I could. Ultimately, he had to choose.

"It sucks, man. Toby's been my best friend since kindergarten."

I almost asked him if the guy's name was really Toby, but then I decided I didn't want to know. I wanted to tell that punk to leave Payton alone, but Payton had to fight his own battles.

"I know, but people change. Just because he was a good friend before doesn't mean he still is. You can care about him and wish he'd do the right thing, but if he doesn't, that's on him. You can't let him drag you down with him."

Payton hung his head, but he nodded.

"Hey," I said and waited until he looked up. "Listen, you can call me. If you need help or you make a bad choice or whatever. You can call me. I'll be there." The kid had two older brothers, but they'd moved out. He had Jordan, too, but sisters were different. If Payton needed me, I'd do what I could to help him.

"Thanks, man." Payton held out his fist.

I tapped it and turned back to my guitar. "Let's go over that last part again. I think you've almost got it."

CHAPTER FIFTEEN

Jordan

I hated myself for the resentment I felt every time I saw Asher's name and not mine on the list on Dad's door. I pushed the feelings down and tried to act like I didn't care. At the end of every game, Asher waited for me outside the locker room with this anxious expression that only made me feel smaller.

I played in every game. I had an amazing boyfriend. What more could I ask for?

"Jordan!" my mom called up the stairs. "Asher's here."

Time to put on my happy face. We were going to the concert in the park tonight. Asher and the guys had been practicing and warming up for the last couple of hours at Jarom's house, but now he needed to head over to the park. He'd insisted on giving me a ride so we could leave together at the end. Natalie and Kelly planned to meet us there and keep me company while the guys played.

I took one last look at myself in the mirror. Asher claimed to love my style, but I didn't miss how all the girls at school looked at him and then looked at me. I knew they wondered why he wanted to be with a girl like me and sometimes, so did I. But I refused to change. Any guy who liked me would have to like, or at least accept, all of me. I couldn't lose myself to please some boy. I wouldn't.

So, I ran downstairs wearing a loose pair of overalls with a long-sleeved graphic t-shirt underneath, hot pink Chucks, and a backward baseball cap I'd found in Bobby's room after he moved out. I only ever wore mascara, and I'd pulled my hair into a low ponytail.

"There you are. Asher's had to make small talk with your dad," Mom teased with a wink at Asher.

"I'm always up to talk hockey, Mrs. Parks," Asher replied.

I shook my head. Suck-up.

"You guys have fun." Dad stood up from where he'd been sitting on the back of the couch. "Kelly and Natalie are meeting you there?"

"Yeah, so I don't have to be by myself when Mr. Rock Star here is on stage." I rubbed Asher's shoulder.

He rolled his eyes before addressing my dad. "We shouldn't be too late. I think the guys want to get something to eat after our set. But we should be done by nine, so, not late."

"Just be home by midnight," Dad said.

"Have fun. And good luck, Asher. Maybe I can talk Coach into going to the park a little later to hear you guys."

Asher's ears turned red. "Oh, well. Yeah, that would be cool."

Mom grinned as I grabbed Asher's hand. Time to leave.

"See you guys later," I called over my shoulder as I pushed Asher out the door.

"Your dad's going to go to the concert," Asher muttered on the way to his car.

"Don't be dramatic." We got into the car then Asher hurried to back out of the driveway.

"Dramatic? Do you know how much balls it took to ask out my Coach's daughter?" he asked.

"Seriously? You didn't act like it."

He glanced at me. "Are you kidding? I thought everyone could see me shaking that first practice after we'd been making out in the back-yard and your dad flipped the lights on and off. I thought for sure I was a dead man."

"I think it helps you live so close. He knows where you sleep. And you know he knows."

Asher's mouth dropped open a little. "That's terrifying."

I rolled my eyes. "It's too late to lose your nerve now, buddy. So, buck up."

The park had already filled with people by the time we arrived. Bands had been scheduled all day, but the more popular groups had been scheduled for the evening. Breakout was a crowd favorite.

Asher parked on a side street and then held my hand as we walked toward a cluster of tents set up behind the sound stage.

"How much longer until you meet the guys?"

"I need to go straight there. Are Natalie and Kelly here yet?"

I checked my phone for messages. "Yeah. They're over by the t-shirt vendors."

Asher kissed the side of my head. "It's called merch."

"Oh, excuse me." I bumped him with my hip.

"I'll walk you over to them and then go find Jarom."

"It's okay. I can find them on my own. You're getting antsy. Just go. I'll see you when you get done."

Asher hesitated. "I have enough time."

"Don't be silly. I'm fine. I know you have stuff to do before you guys go on."

Asher pulled me to a stop. "You'll be front and center so I can find you?"

"Screaming my head off like a groupie." I slid my arms around his neck. "Kiss for luck?"

"If you're offering." He lowered his head.

"I a-" his mouth covered mine.

"Meet me by that blue tent when I'm done?" he asked much too soon.

"Mmhmm."

He kissed me with his smile. "I have to go."

"Okay, okay."

We split, Asher to find the rest of his band, me to find my friends. Natalie had a game earlier while Kelly had a meet. I would have gone to the volleyball game, but we had a game, too.

"Hey, girl!" Natalie called out as soon as she spotted me.

"How was your game?" I asked.

"We won."

"We did, too," Kelly said, holding up a black shirt with a logo for an indie band on the front. "I think I'm gonna get this one."

"How about you? Did you guys win?" Natalie asked me while Kelly paid.

I nodded. "Yeah, we wiped the ice with them. Three to zip."

"Nice."

"You excited to hear your boy sing?" Kelly asked as she tucked her new t-shirt under her arm.

"I hear them sing almost every day." I heard Asher every day, at least.

"This'll be different. Live music with all the equipment and the crowd. It's incredible," Natalie said.

I shrugged. I had no idea if it would be different or not. I knew I'd love it no matter what.

"I'm going to get some cotton candy. I'll be right back." Natalie squeezed her way through the crush of people to a stand selling bags of cotton candy. Several people waited in line. She'd be a minute.

"How are things going with you two, anyway?" Kelly asked.

"Who? Asher and me?"

Kelly nodded.

"Fine. Great. Why do you ask?"

"I don't know. It's been a while since we talked, and I just, you know, wondered..." her voice trailed off, and I felt myself get a little edgy.

"Wondered what?"

"It's nothing. I'm happy for you."

I turned to face her, frowning. "Kelly, what are you talking about? Why would there be anything wrong between Asher and me?"

Kelly bit her lip, looking worried. "I shouldn't have even said anything. We just haven't talked in so long."

I put my hand on my hip and glared at her. "Kelly!"

She held up her hands in surrender. "It's just I have a few classes with him, and I see him in the halls. Your schedule is so different.

You're never nearby. He always has girls hanging all over him. I don't think he encourages them, but he doesn't push them away, either."

What?

"What do you mean 'hanging all over him'? What does that mean? Like touching him?"

Kelly's face contorted. "I shouldn't have said anything. It's probably nothing."

"Probably?" I wanted to throw up. Other girls had their hands on my boyfriend! And he let them? What the hell!

"What's going on?" Natalie asked as she stuffed a fluffy glob of cotton candy into her mouth.

"What's going on is my best friend just told me my boyfriend's a cheater!" I cried then spun on my heel to get away from them.

"I never said that!" Kelly grabbed my arm.

"Then what did you say? What did you mean? You obviously wanted to warn me about something." I couldn't believe this. Hot tears pricked my eyes.

"Jordan, I thought you knew. Asher's hot. He's in a band. He's new and mysterious. You don't think girls at school throw themselves at him?" Kelly folded her arms over her stomach. "I just, you don't see him at school very much."

I glanced at Natalie. "You see him, too?"

Natalie grimaced. "Sometimes. But it's not like he's flirting." She gave Kelly a hard look making me wonder if they'd discussed whether or not to mention any of this to me, and Kelly had gone rogue by saying something. "He's nice. And it's not like it's his fault he's good-looking and girls like him."

My head hurt.

My heart hurt.

Asher's song cut through the hurt just enough for me to realize we needed to go. "I have to go. I promised Asher I'd be upfront where he could see me."

Without waiting to see if my friends would follow, I wove my way through the throngs of people toward the stage. How long ago had it been? Ten minutes since I'd seen him? Fifteen since he kissed me?

It took most of the first song for me to push my way to the front of the crowd. I didn't even realize I had tears streaming down my cheeks until I looked up at him. He'd been searching for me, I could tell. His eyes lit when he saw me, but then almost immediately he frowned, searching my face. That's when I lifted my hands to my cheeks and felt the moisture there.

I thought he might jump from the stage before finishing his song, but he didn't. His eyes never left mine, and when the song ended, he spoke to the crowd.

"Thanks for being here. I'm Asher. And we're Breakout. Jarom, Adam, and Bash back there on drums." His voice sounded smooth and confident. Next to me, a group of girls pushed me aside, screaming and yelling Asher's name. He smiled at them briefly before his eyes found me again. "I'd like to give a shout-out to my girl. This one's for you, babe."

Asher

I sang my heart out to Jordan and somehow managed not to jump into the crowd to find out why she had tears streaming down her face. She cried through our entire set. And not the groupie I love you kind of cry, the heartbroken kind.

Natalie and Kelly stood beside her, but her eyes never left me as I tried to engage with the crowd. Those were the longest twenty minutes of my life. Near the end of the last song, I begged her with my eyes to wait for me after.

Once we finished, I wanted to leap off the front of the stage to get to Jordan, but the stage manager shuffled us offstage, leaving me no choice but to follow him. I craned my neck to keep an eye on Jordan, but Jarom wasn't having it.

"Dude, that was so sick! Did you see all those girls, man?" He grabbed my shoulders and shook. "They loved you!"

"Guys, I gotta run." Much as I wanted to celebrate with them, I had to find Jordan. "I have to find Jordan."

"Yeah, what's up with her? Was she crying?" Adam asked.

But Jarom shook his head. "Man, are you crazy? Look at all these fans. You can't leave now."

I set my jaw. "I'm finding Jordan."

Jarom held up his hands. The stage manager herded us to a set of stairs leading off the stage to the tents that had served as dressing rooms for the different acts. I pushed to the front to go down the stairs first, but at the bottom, a huge crowd had formed.

And they were all girls.

"Asher!"

"Asher, you're so hot!"

There were a few shout-outs to the other guys as well, but each time a girl called my name, it felt like a direct hit. Because none of them were Jordan.

"Asher, who's your girlfriend? I bet I can take her!"

My eyes widened at that one. There were so many girls, I'd never get past them. Searching over their heads, I looked for Jordan by the blue tent. And I found her. Waiting. Watching. Crying. I lifted my hand, signaling for her to stay. She shook her head. Panic filled my chest.

"Jordan!" She couldn't hear me, but that didn't keep me from calling out again. I fought my way through the girls who clawed at my clothes. My bandmates followed close behind, laughing and signing autographs like we were celebrities or something. This was a concert in the park, for goodness sake!

By the time I got away from the crowd and made it to the tent, Jordan was gone.

Feeling more desperate than ever, I sprinted toward my car, searching every face I passed for the one I wanted.

"Asher!"

Crap. My dad. I forgot he and Shari were going to be there. I stopped and turned around. They were walking my way, Caleb, in an infant carrier strapped to my dad's chest. His arms and legs flapped when he saw me. As much as I wanted to keep running, I had to talk to them. I almost couldn't believe Shari talked my dad into coming.

"Asher, you guys were amazing." Shari wrapped me in a hug.

"Weren't they, Derek? You were so good." She shook her head like she couldn't believe it, but her eyes shone with pride.

"Thanks. That means a lot."

Dad still hadn't said anything. I turned to him, focusing my attention on my little brother.

"Hey, buddy. Did you like my music? Yeah?" He grabbed onto my finger. "You're my biggest fan, huh?"

Caleb gurgled. "Uh!" he shouted. I smiled because that was as close as he could get to say my name.

Dad cleared his throat, effectively killing my smile. I stood up straight and met his gaze.

"You guys sounded good, Ash."

Wow.

And he didn't even appear to be choking on the words.

"Thanks, Dad."

The moment turned awkward. Of course, Shari stepped in to save the day.

"Where's Jordan? I thought she was here with you?"

"Oh, um," I reached my hand up to the back of my neck. "We got separated. I was looking for her when I ran into you guys." They didn't need the gory details.

Shari frowned, her eyes darting around, looking for Jordan herself. "Well, you should go find her. Who knows who's at this thing. You shouldn't leave her alone."

I didn't want to. Leaving her alone was the last thing I wanted. "I'm sorry to rush off. But you're right. I should go find her." I started to move away. "I'll see you guys later. Thanks for coming!" I called over my shoulder, taking off at a run, my mind once again going to what had happened.

We were good. Everything was fine when I left her. Less than an hour ago, my life was about as perfect as it could get.

The whole way to my car, I kept hoping she'd be there waiting for me, but that would have been too easy. Something had happened. Somehow, I'd hurt her, and I didn't have any idea how. But it happened in the fifteen minutes between leaving her to find the band and her arriving to hear me sing. What could I have done in that amount of time? We weren't even together!

My mind raced through all the possibilities. She'd been with her friends. What did they have to do with me? Had I offended one of them? Had they told her something? But what?

I had to find her. But where?

By the time I reached my car, I figured there was only one place.

When I got home, Dad and Shari were still gone.

I bypassed the house and headed straight into the backyard.

"Jordan!" I wanted to collapse with relief. Instead, I ran to her. "Jordan," I breathed her name again when she didn't push me away because I had to hold her. "What happened? Why are you crying? I've been so scared."

Her arms came around my waist. Her body shook with emotion.

I held her as long as I could until I had to see her face, her eyes. "Please, tell me."

"I'm so stupid." Her red, watery eyes closed tight, forcing tears down her cheeks.

"No. I know you, and you aren't stupid. Whatever it is-" I'd do anything to comfort her. Knowing I craved the connection and hoping she did, too, I kissed her softly. I should have kept it short, but didn't. Couldn't. For several moments we shared sweet, tender kisses.

Jordan pulled away first, but not before wiping her tears on my shirt. I had to smile at that, but it was short-lived.

"Let's sit down." Taking her hands in mine, I led her to the wrought iron love seat. "Will you tell me what's going on?"

She buried her face in her hands. "I feel so stupid."

"Jordan, come on." I pulled her hands down. "What happened?"

"I was talking to Kelly."

I knew it had to do with her friends! But what?

"And?"

Jordan swallowed and had a hard time meeting my eyes. "Kelly said she's seen you."

"Okay?" I saw Kelly every day. We had a couple of classes together. Not to mention the times I saw her when we were both with Jordan.

"She said she's seen you with other girls."

Whoa.

What?

I felt as though I'd been kicked in the gut.

I shook my head. "Jordan, no. Are you kidding?" I could just shake Kelly for trying to come between us like this. "I haven't even looked at another girl since the first day of school when you yelled at me for parking in your spot."

Jordan pushed herself out of my grasp, but she didn't get up. I let my hands fall into my lap and ordered them not to touch her until I knew, without a doubt, she wanted them to.

"Kelly said girls hang all over you and flirt with you all the time, and I never see it because we don't have any classes together."

Oh.

My damned cheeks flushed. Of course, she noticed.

"It's true!" Jordan jumped to her feet.

I hurried to join her. "No! At least, not the way Kelly presented it." I covered my face with my hand. "Girls like me. Or they like the way I look. I never encourage any of them, but it's true, they always try to hang around me. Short of being a complete jerk to everyone I meet, what am I supposed to do?"

Jordan slammed her hands onto her hips. "Um, you could start by telling them you have a girlfriend?"

"You think I don't do that? I'd announce it over the PA system if I thought it would help." Gah, that made me sound so arrogant.

"Right. I bet it bothers you to have girls falling at your feet. Just like at the concert." Jordan's accusation stung.

I thought about all the girls who flirted with me at school, and the times I'd caught Ms. Jackson blushing around me. She wasn't the only one. I'd been approached by perfect strangers. Propositioned. Handed business cards by talent agents looking for models. I even had an ex-girlfriend back in Minnesota whose mom came on to me more than once.

This wasn't new. It likely wouldn't get any better. Especially, if I had my way and made something of myself with my music. I'd seen it earlier that night. People who'd been milling around talking or shopping at the vendor tables stopped to listen to Breakout. Once we'd finished our set, we'd drawn the biggest crowd that day, according to the event organizer who'd informed us as we exited the stage.

A million different thoughts ran through my mind as I stared at her. All my life, I'd been struggling for acceptance. Not because of my mom and her fame. Not because of my appearance or my talent. Not because of my abilities on the ice.

Because of me.

Asher.

I had the same insecurities as anyone.

I'd been objectified. Used. Discarded by my own mother. Manipulated by my father. And now Jordan wanted to accuse me of being what? Kind?

So, I smiled at the girls who listened to my music. I didn't act like a jerk at school to my peers. I tried to be a good son and brother. I'd even been a friend to her brother!

If that made me a horrible boyfriend…Well, then I was a horrible boyfriend.

"I've never given you a reason not to trust me, Jordan." My heart hurt. But I wouldn't beg.

A mix of emotions passed through her eyes. She still held herself away from me.

My phone vibrated in my pocket. On instinct, I reached for it. Jordan's gaze followed my hand. I moved to put it back in my pocket without really looking at it when a name on the screen caught my eye.

Crap.

I had to check. What if…

"I have to get this. It's-" I couldn't tell her who had texted me. I bit the inside of my cheek. Double crap.

Jordan rolled her eyes and jumped to her feet.

I opened the message, reading it as my stomach dropped to my toes.

I slipped my phone back into my jeans and stood. "I have to go."

"Where? Don't you think we should work this out?"

I exhaled. "I didn't do anything wrong, Jordan. I might not handle every situation the right way, but I haven't done anything I'm ashamed of with any girl at school or anywhere else."

She glanced at my phone. "And that?"

I closed my eyes, knowing she wouldn't let it go. "I can't tell you."

Her mouth dropped open before she snapped it closed. "Fine."

My jaw clenched. I wanted to tell her. So badly. But I couldn't. Not without breaking a promise.

"Fine."

I told Jordan the truth. And she still didn't trust me. I wouldn't lose the trust of someone else to gain her's back.

"You should go then."

"And this?" I asked, gesturing between us.

Her arms folded over her stomach, making her look small. "I don't know. Maybe we need a break."

"Right." I nodded to myself as I turned away from her. Right. "I'll see you around, Jordan."

CHAPTER SIXTEEN

Jordan

He walked away. He just walked away.

I went home and cried myself to sleep. I couldn't remember the last time I did that. Not since I'd reached double-digit age. And I felt mortified to be crying over a boy. I wanted to scream.

At myself.

But maybe it just meant I had real feelings for Asher. It kind of blew my mind because it didn't seem that long ago I thought I hated him. But what did it mean? I cared about him. I liked him. But what about the things he'd told me the night before? And what Kelly said about him and other girls? Did I believe Asher that he didn't encourage them? And even if he didn't, could I be okay in a relationship with someone who attracted so much attention? I'd been there the night before. The audience loved Breakout. They were good. They were more than good. And they were all good-looking. Gorgeous, even. What if Asher's dreams were like his mom's dreams to make it big?

I didn't have any delusions. I'd been dating Asher for just a short time, but I did have feelings for him. I wanted things to work out between us. Could I handle it if he became famous? If what happened last night was just the beginning?

I didn't have the answers. And I didn't know if I trusted him. He never called or texted after he left me last night. He refused to tell me where he was going or what he was doing. I hated the way it made me feel, distrusting, unsettled, insecure. Those weren't the best emotions in a relationship. If we even had a relationship anymore.

The next morning I woke up to a quiet house. Mom and Dad left a note on the counter saying they'd gone to breakfast and then to the home improvement store. They'd be gone for most of the day. Payton had been allowed to sleep over at his friend Tyler's house for the first time in ages, and he hadn't made it home yet.

The hot chocolate packets in the pantry were calling my name. I checked the fridge for cream before taking a pot down from the rack hanging from the ceiling to fill with water. The kitchen faced the backyard and the window over the sink gave me a perfect view of-

Payton?

The pot fell from my hand, clattering into the sink. What the heck? Why on earth was my little brother leaving the Sloane's house?

Abandoning all thoughts of hot chocolate, I swung open the back door and marched outside. Payton's head jerked toward me, a look of alarm on his face.

"What are you doing? You're supposed to be at Tyler's." I was yelling. Who could blame me? "Why are you coming out of Asher's house?"

Payton scowled. "None of your business. Why are you even awake? You never get up before noon on Sunday."

Truth. But I had a hard time sleeping after last night.

I put my hands on my hips. "Not the point. Do Mom and Dad know where you are?"

Payton's jaw tightened. "No. And they don't need to know." He pointed a finger at me. "And if they find out, I'll know you were the one to tell them."

"So what? They deserve to know if you're doing something you shouldn't."

"Hey! Hey! What's going on out here?" Asher came striding across

the yard wearing a concerned expression and looking incredibly sexy in an I-just-woke-up kind of way.

I whirled toward him, ignoring my lustful thoughts because he'd become enemy number one again. "You!" I poked his chest. "What are you doing with my brother? He's supposed to be at his friend's house."

Asher glanced at Payton. Some kind of silent communication passed between them, making me angrier.

I poked Asher again. "You were supposed to help him!"

Asher caught my finger in his hand. "I have been helping him."

"Oh, really? How? And how did he get here?" I thought back to the night before and the text message on Asher's phone. The one he wouldn't tell me about. The one he left me for. "It was Payton? On your phone last night?"

Asher's lips pressed together.

I turned to Payton. "You texted him? Why?"

"Butt out, Jordan. This has nothing to do with you."

"You're my brother! And you." I turned back to Asher. "You're supposed to be my friend."

Asher's eyes narrowed. "Friend? That's what this has been, Jordan? Friends."

I shrank back a little from the rancor in his tone. "Not anymore, it isn't."

Asher reared back as though I'd slapped him. And I might as well have for how awful I felt as soon as the words left my mouth.

"Asher—"

"No." He put his hands out to stop me. "No. You don't trust me enough to believe in me, and you're right. I don't need *friends* like that." He looked to Payton. "I'll see you tomorrow, man. Remember what we talked about."

Payton nodded while I struggled to breathe.

What had I just done?

Asher walked away. Without a backward glance, he left me standing there with my brother.

"Nice one, Jord." Payton shook his head, and then he left me, too.

How did things get to be such a mess?

Slowly, I followed my brother into the house. He'd already gone upstairs. I heard the shower going. No longer feeling like having hot chocolate, I grabbed a half-eaten container of ice cream from the freezer in the basement and settled onto the oversized beanbag chair in front of the television.

Thank goodness for the Hallmark Channel.

The next morning, I didn't wait around to see if Asher would stop by to pick me up for school. I knew he wouldn't. I tried not to look for his car in the parking lot, but my brain had already been conditioned to find it. My stomach fluttered even though I knew I probably wouldn't see him.

Natalie and Kelly had been calling and texting me since the concert on Saturday, but I'd been ignoring them. When Natalie approached me, it was with some trepidation. I didn't miss the way her eyes flicked to the empty space on either side of me— Asher had been filling one or the other for weeks now— or how her face fell to find him missing.

"What happened?" she asked.

"Nothing. We broke up." And I'd been crying for almost forty-eight hours, but why dwell on that? Or admit to it?

"What? Why?" Natalie thought Kelly exaggerated Asher's interactions with his fan club. She called it *being nice*, while Kelly insisted he'd been flirting. At this point, I didn't know what to think, other than I missed him.

And I'd screwed things up.

I shrugged. "It doesn't matter. It's over."

"What's over?" Kelly asked, and I barely hid my irritation. I should just wait to say anything to Natalie until Kelly showed up. Every morning we had to rehash the first five minutes of conversation Kelly missed.

"She broke up with Asher," Natalie said.

Kelly frowned. "What? Really? Because of what I told you?"

"What did you think would happen?" I asked.

Kelly blinked. "I don't know. I guess I thought you guys would talk and there would be some other explanation."

I rounded on her. "If that's what you thought, then why didn't you find out yourself before making me doubt my boyfriend?"

Kelly's mouth dropped open. "Hey, I was just looking out for you!"

"What happened, Kel? Why do you think every guy's a douche? Asher's not like that. And now he hates me!"

"You didn't have to go accusing him of anything, Jordan. You could have just asked him. Talked to him. But you didn't. You got your feelings hurt and ran off crying. Did you even let him explain? Hmm. I didn't think so. So, don't go blaming me for what you did. All I did was give you the information. You didn't have to believe me, and you didn't have to push him away." With that, Kelly turned on her heel and walked away, leaving me with my mouth hanging open.

Well, crap.

"I gotta go," I told Natalie. "I'll see you later."

But I didn't. For the next couple of weeks, I avoided Natalie and Kelly, choosing to pack my lunch and eat it in the commons. I went to practice, worked on speed training in the basement, and then locked myself away in my bedroom.

I'd alienated both of my best friends. My boyfriend. And my little brother.

And every night, I opened my window. But Asher never sang.

Asher

"You miss her, don't you?"

"Who?" But I knew exactly.

Payton rolled his eyes. "Jordan, you idiot. You miss her."

I didn't answer. I didn't need to. You didn't have to know me well to know I was miserable. It had been over two weeks since the argument in her backyard, both of them.

"I feel bad, though. Like it's my fault. If you hadn't covered for me-"

"Dude, it's not like that. There was other stuff, too." I stood to pack up my guitar. I needed to head back over to the high school. We were days away from the talent show, and Payton had been working his tail off. He'd learned a song to sing on his own, and then we'd worked on one to perform together.

"Other stuff like what?" he asked.

Payton and I had gotten pretty tight lately, but not that tight. "Dude, I'm not talking about your sister with you."

"But you still like her, don't you? And I know for a fact she likes you back."

I stopped to look over at him. "How do you know she still likes me?"

Payton groaned as he rolled his eyes this time. "Are you kidding me? All she's done is mope around for two solid weeks. She stares out the window at your house all the time. And her room has a permanent draft coming under the door because her window's always open."

I didn't know if I should believe him. Jordan had done a bang-up job of ignoring me. We avoided eye contact during practice, only speaking when necessary. Which didn't happen often. I hardly ever saw her at school, even when I went looking.

And what did I think about her opening her window?

I didn't have the heart to play outside anymore. The alcove between the trees had become our spot. Mine, and Jordan's. I didn't want to go out there anymore without her. But even if she did miss me, so what? She didn't tell me. She didn't apologize for not trusting me, for accusing me of basically cheating on her.

"It doesn't matter, Pay. She doesn't trust me. What can I do about that? She thinks I'm lying to her. Hiding things. And I'm not."

Payton frowned. "Well, you are hiding what happened with me, right?"

"Well, yeah, but how can get her trust by breaking yours? It doesn't work like that. Besides, I wouldn't go behind your back like that, man. We're buds, right?" I held out my fist.

Payton hesitated. But then he grinned. "Yeah, we are." He bumped his fist on the top, then the bottom, of mine.

"Good. Now, I gotta get back to school." I headed to the door but called over my shoulder. "Keep practicing."

"Hey, wait!" Payton called out.

I stopped and turned around. "What?"

He jogged over to the door. "What about the ticket?"

I frowned. "What do you mean?"

"Dude, the one for Jordan? What are you going to do if we don't take her?"

Hmm. I hadn't thought about it. "I don't know. Take Jarom?"

Payton made a face. "Okay, but don't tell him yet. Wait and see if things work out first with you and Jordan."

I ran my fingers through my hair and sighed. "Payton, I don't think-"

"Promise. Please. Just wait. See what happens?"

I could tell it was important to him, so I agreed. "Fine. I'll wait. But I don't think anything will change between Jordan and me."

Payton grinned. "I wouldn't be so sure about that, man."

"Okay, weirdo. I have to go." I reached out and ruffled his hair, which I knew he hated and hurried out the door before he could catch me.

Payton

I had to do something. As much as I might not always show it, I loved my sister. As far as sisters went, I probably had one of the coolest. How many guys could say they had a badass sister who played hockey on a guys' team?

Not many.

And she must be pretty, or a guy like Asher wouldn't look twice at her. I could only dream of being as cool as him.

So, I figured, I'd better fix the part of them that broke because of me. I owed it to Asher, and if I'm honest, I owed it to Jordan. Asher told me what she'd done. How it had been her idea for him to mentor me. At first, it kind of made me mad, like he was only my friend because of my sister, but then I realized I didn't care. I loved playing the guitar, and I didn't suck at singing. Whatever his motivations were in the beginning, I knew he was my friend now.

So, I needed to tell Jordan what happened that night, and if she still wanted to be mad at Asher, well, at least, it wouldn't be because of me.

After dinner, I knocked on Jordan's bedroom door. The cold air from under her door chilled my bare toes. Man, she had it bad.

"Jordan, come on. I need to talk to you." I knocked again.

"Hang on. I'm coming." She opened the door, and I laughed out loud.

"What are you wearing?"

Her cheeks got red as she folded her arms over the unicorn onesie costume she'd worn for Halloween a couple of years ago. "I was a little chilly."

I gave her a knowing look and walked into her room. "I wonder why." I closed the window and pulled the curtains shut over it.

She frowned. "What are you doing?" She started to move toward it, but I stopped her.

"He's not there. One, it's freezing. And two, didn't you two used to make out back there?" I shuddered just thinking about it. Gross. "He's not going to sit there and be reminded of that."

Her shoulders fell.

"This is cute, though." I touched the arm of her costume. "You should wear it to school."

She shoved my hand away. "Shut up, you punk. What are you doing here, anyway?" She dropped onto her bed, snuggling into her pillows and blankets.

I sat down beside her and reminded myself I had to do this. I owed it to Asher. And I owed it to Jordan. If I'm honest, I should go downstairs after and tell my parents, too. Hmmm. Maybe not.

"I have something I need to tell you. About that night, when I texted Asher." Now, I had her attention. Jordan sat up and scooted back to lean against her headboard.

"What? Why? Did he tell you to?" she asked.

I shook my head. "No. Of course not."

"Then why are you doing it?"

I exhaled a deep breath. "Because it's the right thing to do. You ready?"

She nodded.

"Okay, so you know I was supposed to spend the night at Tyler's that night?" She nodded again. "Yeah, well, um..." I hated admitting this to her because it meant she'd been right all along. Not about Tyler, about me. "So, you know we've been buds forever, but he's been getting into things he shouldn't and trying to drag me down with him. I told Asher about it one day when we were at mentoring and he told me to cut Tyler loose. He didn't say it like that, but that's what he meant. And I was going to. That night when he asked if I could spend the night. I planned to talk to him and say we couldn't be friends anymore if he didn't straighten up. When we spoke that night, he was like, yeah, cool, fine. And I thought, *whew*, you know. Because I didn't want to lose my friend.

"Well, then he's like, let's go to the corner store and get some snacks, right? So, we did, but when we got there, he didn't want to pay for anything. He started acting like he was going to steal all this crap from the convenience store."

"Payton!" Jordan sat up and put her hand on my arm.

"I know! Jord, I already got picked up by the police this summer. They told me one more screwup and I was going to juvie. Since I've been hanging out with Asher, I don't know, he's pretty cool, and he's teaching me to play. I've been talking to some guys about starting a band of our own. I can't do that if I'm in juvie."

"So, what did you do?"

"I ran. I ran as fast as I could. I didn't want to be anywhere near that place if Tyler got caught. All he would have to do is say I was there, too, and I'd be done. So, as soon as I got far enough away, I texted Asher to come and pick me up."

CHAPTER SEVENTEEN

Jordan

I sat back against my headboard. "Why didn't you call me? Or Mom and Dad?"

Payton made a face. "Seriously? Do you know what would have happened if I called Mom and Dad? I didn't even do anything. As far as I know, Tyler didn't either. At least, not that time."

"Well, what about Joe? Or Bobby?"

Payton leaned back with a groan. "Jordan, don't be stupid. They live forever away. It was late at night. Asher said I could call him, so I did. I needed help, and he helped me. He took me back to his house so Mom and Dad wouldn't ask any questions. I haven't talked to Tyler since then. It's done. I didn't do anything bad, except stay the night somewhere safe rather than with my ex-friend who's a delinquent."

It made sense. And really, how could I be mad at him? He was twelve, and he needed help.

"Okay. Fine. I get it. But why didn't he tell me?"

"Jordan, come on! Bro code. I asked him not to tell you, and he didn't."

I so wanted to be mad at Asher. I wanted this to be his fault and not mine for jumping to conclusions.

"Look, sis. Asher and I are kinda friends now, but he did all this for you. Not for me."

I scowled at my little brother. Punk kid.

"Guess what he said to me today."

"What?" I asked sulking.

"He said he couldn't earn your trust by breaking mine." Payton stood up and stretched. "If you ask me, Jord, he's a good guy, and you're an idiot if you don't want to be his girlfriend. The dude's a rock star."

Gah! I hated he was right. "But that's kind of the problem. Kelly said he has girls hanging all over him all the time." I had no idea why I told my brother that, but we were sharing, and it just slipped out.

"Of course, he does! So does Joe. And Bobby. But that doesn't mean they're players." Payton made a face as he sat back down. "Okay, maybe Bobby is a little bit. But he's not a jerk. And neither is Asher. I think he cares about you, Jord. The guy's been miserable. I can hardly stand being around him, he's so mopey."

"He is?" I hoped I didn't sound too hopeful.

Payton smirked. "Yes. And it sucks. We've been working together a lot because the talent show's this weekend, and he's hard to deal with right now."

I bit my lip to keep my grin under control. Could it be possible? Did Asher miss me as much as I missed him? And would he forgive me? I wanted him to, but that would require apologizing. But how?

"Thanks, Payton. You didn't owe me an explanation, but I'm glad you told me." Leaning over, I hugged him.

"Ugh. Why are you hugging me?" he asked while hugging me back.

"Because I love you, too." I ruffled his hair.

He smacked my hand away and stood up. "I'm leaving. And don't ever touch me again."

"See you later, Pay!" I yelled after him as he slammed my door shut behind him.

Sitting back on my bed, I stared at my closed-up window and thought about how I could fix things with Asher. I knew I needed to apologize to him. But would a simple apology be enough, or did I need to come up with something better? I had no idea, but I knew that's all I would be thinking about until one came to me.

Friday.

The next night was the talent show. But first, we had a game. I arrived at the rink early, before anybody else except my dad.

"Jordan, what are you doing here so early?" Dad asked when I stuck my head inside his office without looking at the starting lineup. It never changed, so I didn't bother looking. "Come in, sit down."

I did as he asked, taking a seat in the cracked pleather chair in front of his desk. "I wasn't doing anything at home, so I figured I'd get a head start warming up."

Dad sat back, his fingers steepled in front of his face as he studied me. "Did you check the list?"

I shook my head. "Nope."

He raised his brows. "No? Why not?"

My heart lurched a little. "Because it's the same every week. Why? Should I?" I started to lift out of my chair.

"Wait!" Dad stopped me. "Yes, you should look, but first, I want to talk to you about something."

I sat back down, but I didn't want to. Dang! Why didn't I look at the list before walking in? How would I ever sit through one of Dad's talks while wondering what was on that piece of paper?

Dad didn't say anything right away, and when he did, I couldn't believe the words coming out of his mouth. "I didn't tell you this when you asked me to join the team, but I already knew Asher would be transferring here."

"I'm sorry, what?" I had to be hearing things.

"Asher Sloane is one of the best left-wings in the northeast. I recruited him."

He'd recruited Asher? "But, but why?" I didn't understand. "You encouraged me to leave my team. You let me go through all of that just to ride the bench." I stood up, my fists clenched at my sides. "How could you do that?"

Dad stood, too, and walked around to the front of his desk. "What have I always taught you, Jordan?"

"Play to win," I repeated the mantra without even thinking.

Dad nodded. "Play to win. Every decision I make for this team is to that end. Winning games. This isn't pee-wee's, kiddo. My players move out and up."

"I know that!"

Dad's lips thinned at my outburst.

"Sorry, sir."

"Jordan, if your team had been competitive, if I saw you improve by leaps and bounds each season, I would have never encouraged you to move to my team. I don't enjoy watching you get pushed around by these guys who are a lot bigger than you. But I know your dream, sweetheart. I know you want to keep playing, and this was the only way I could help you."

"By bringing in someone better than me, so I'd hardly ever get to play!" I bit my lip. I'd yelled at him again.

Dad looked down at his feet and sighed, weighing his words while I waited. Finally, he met my gaze. "No. I brought Asher here to make you better. I knew if you had to compete every week for the starting position, you would. I knew you'd work your butt off to play better than him. And you have."

I scoffed. "I'm never going to be better than him. You just said he's the best left-wing in the northeast!"

Dad nodded. "He is. And maybe you won't ever play as well as him, but you are playing better than you ever have before. And you're playing better than Justin Painter."

"Justin? You're going to put me in as defenseman?" Seriously?

"No. I'm going to put Asher in as left defense and you in for left-wing. Between the two of you, you're both better than Justin. Even if you weren't left-handed. Justin doesn't want it bad enough. Maybe if he worked harder— but that's a conversation for him."

I stared at him, stunned. "Are you serious? You're starting me?"

"Yes, Jordan. You're starting."

I threw my arms around his neck and whooped. "Thank you, Daddy! Thank you!"

Dad laughed as he hugged me back. "Don't thank me. Whatever you and Asher have been working on in the basement's been making a difference."

I pulled back with a frown. Really? I owed this to him, too? Even though Asher and I hadn't been working out together, I'd been doing the things he showed me on my own. And it made enough of a difference I'd reached my goal to start in a game this season.

"Hey, what's the matter?" Dad brushed his thumbs over my cheeks.

"Asher."

Understanding washed over Dad's face. "Do I need to get involved? Did he hurt you?"

I shook my head. "No, this one's on me, I'm afraid."

Dad lifted one brow. "Well, you'll make it right."

I only hoped he was right.

I barely remembered changing in the locker room. I waited for Dad to give me the signal to enter the locker room for the pre-game pep talk. I walked in to find the only open seat between Leo and Asher. Excitement over getting to start couldn't entirely dispel the awkwardness of having to sit beside my recent ex-boyfriend, who also happened to be my biggest competition on the team.

But not anymore. Tonight we both got to start. We'd be on the ice at the same time. Playing to win.

Asher

She made me crazy. I missed her so much. I wanted to blow off this game and fix everything broken between us, but of course, I wouldn't. Tonight Jordan's goal became a reality. I found myself grinning like a fool when I spotted her name on the starting roster earlier. I didn't even mind Coach bumping me from winger to defense if it meant Jordan would get to play.

She entered the locker room with her lip tucked between her

teeth. She had to be excited but nervous, too. She sat beside me on the bench, and I clenched my fists to keep my hands from reaching out to her. I wondered if she could hear my heart pounding in my chest.

Coach went through his pre-game spiel. Once he finished, we made our way into the tunnel where Joe got everyone fired up. The announcer called the names of the starters for the opposing team.

"Let's go!" Joe shouted. He turned to Jordan and slapped the top of her helmet. "You got this!"

"JOE PARKS!" the announcer called. Joe skated out onto the ice, his arms raised.

Once again, I couldn't take my eyes off Jordan. She glanced at me and found me watching her. Our eyes held. "Good luck," I said.

She nodded.

"JORDAN PARKS!"

Jordan grinned and, with one last look, followed her brother.

We won. We'd only lost two games so far this season and were on track to make it into the postseason, but that wouldn't be until after New Year's.

I hurried to shower and change in the locker room. I was the first one done, and hopefully, I'd gotten out before Jordan.

Standing outside the women's locker room, I waited. After a few minutes, a locker door slammed from within. I pushed away from the wall to stand up straight. I still had no idea what to say to her, I just knew it had to be something.

Footsteps. A shadow. And suddenly, she stood before me. Her pretty mouth dropped open. My lips tingled.

"Hi." Brilliant opening line.

Jordan blinked. "Hi."

Think fast, Asher!

"I um... good game. I just wanted to say good game." So lame.

Jordan bit her lip. "Thanks. I guess I owe it to you."

"You don't owe me anything." Hadn't I come here to take her place on the team?

She nodded. "I do. Dad said the speed training helped. I think he might even add it to our regular practices."

I shrugged. "I just showed you how to do it. You did all the work."

"Still."

I hated this. But I didn't know what to do. I couldn't make Jordan trust me. I could spend all my time and energy reassuring her, but I didn't want a relationship like that. She had to decide if it was worth the risk. If I was.

"Are you coming to the talent show?" I asked.

A small smile tipped her lips. "Yeah, I'll be there."

"Good. So, I'll see you then?" *Gah, I'm an idiot.*

"I'll see you then."

"Okay." I nodded. Good grief. I needed to get out of there. "Bye."

She grinned. "Bye."

I left before I lost all self-control and begged her to give us a second chance. I wanted to be with her. I cared about her. Heck, I might even love her. All I knew, I was miserable without her.

"Hey, um, can I talk to you about something?" Payton asked. We had about thirty minutes before he would take the stage in the talent show. We'd gone over his song twice and practiced our duet once. Payton sounded awesome. I knew he was ready.

"Yeah, sure. Anything."

He looked nervous like he didn't want to tell me whatever he had to say.

"Dude, it's all good. Just say it."

Payton cleared his throat. "Well, I've been practicing with some guys over at my buddy John's house. We've been working on this song, but we didn't think we'd be ready for the show, so we didn't sign up for a spot."

Ohh. I understood. He wanted to take our spot and go out there with his band. I put my hand on his shoulder.

"Man, this thing isn't about me. If you want to sing with your guys, I think you should do it."

Payton's body sagged with relief. "Really? You don't care?"

"Payton, I don't care at all. This is your chance to show what you've got. If you and your band are ready, then you should do it." I glanced around the band room where the different acts were getting ready. "Are they all here? You guys should run through your song, don't you think?"

Payton nodded. "Yeah, they're over there." He pointed to three kids hovering near the door. He waved and they shuffled their way over. "Guys, this is Asher. Asher, meet John, Scott, and Trey."

We exchanged fist bumps. "Do you want me to listen in while you run through?"

All four heads nodded. "Yeah, man, that would be freaking awesome," Payton's friend John said, looking at me a little awestruck. "We heard you guys in the park a while back."

"Oh, yeah? Cool. Well, let's hear what you've got."

The band room had all the instruments they needed to run through their song. I sat in a chair in front of them and listened while they performed. They weren't half bad. I could tell Payton had passed along a lot of the advice and instruction I'd given him to his friends. They sounded as though they'd put the time in. I wouldn't have to worry about them embarrassing themselves in front of their friends.

"That was incredible," I told them once they finished.

Their faces split into happy grins before they could catch themselves, smoothing their expressions into something a little cooler.

"Payton, my man, I think you are ready. I'm gonna go find a seat, so I don't miss anything."

Payton snorted. "I think you should go and find my sister instead."

A laugh ripped from my throat. "Hey! What are you talking about?"

He gave me a look. "It's okay. You know you want to."

He wasn't wrong. But still. "I want to see you perform, man. I wouldn't miss it."

"Fine. But then, I think you should find Jordan. I can't take much more pouting. From either of you."

My eyes bulged. Who was this kid? "Just go out there and break a leg, okay? Let me worry about Jordan."

"Whatever, man. See you after?" he asked.

"Absolutely."

I left them to wait for their turn onstage. Payton would sing solo first and then perform with his band. I shook my head, thinking about how far he'd come in such a short amount of time. He'd picked up the guitar like a natural. He still had a long way to go, but he could play the chords he needed to sing this song, and after tonight, the pressure would be off. He could learn at his own pace because he wanted to, not because he had to. And I had a feeling he would do it, too.

The middle school auditorium was packed. When I mentioned the talent show to Mr. Hooper, I worried there wouldn't be enough interest. Surprisingly, about twenty acts signed up, and family and friends had shown up to offer their support. Mr. Hooper even told me he planned to add the talent show as a permanent activity for the school each fall.

According to the program, Payton would be up next. I found an empty patch of the wall at the back to lean against and watched a cute little girl juggle eight balls between her legs. I clapped with everyone else when she finished, but as she walked offstage, I became aware of a presence beside me, one I'd know anywhere.

Jordan.

Neither of us said anything. Payton had already walked onstage. As much as I wanted to fix things with his sister, I also wanted to be there for him. I appreciated the friendship we'd developed, and this night represented so much accomplishment for both of us.

That didn't mean I wasn't completely aware of every minute brush of my arm against Jordan's or how, after the third time we touched, she shifted, so her shoulder pressed against mine.

Dang.

My heart raced as Payton settled on a stool and adjusted the guitar in his lap. He fiddled with the microphone and the auditorium filled with a loud screech.

"Oh, uh, sorry," he muttered. An amused murmur rose from the audience. And even from the back wall, I saw the red creeping up his neck, but he smiled and didn't let it fluster him too much.

Payton introduced himself and the song he'd be singing. Then his fingers strummed the first chord. And I'd never felt so proud.

About halfway through his song, Jordan's hand slid through the crook in my arm. I glanced over to find her determinedly keeping her eyes on her brother. Still, she couldn't hide her pulse thrumming wildly, almost as violently as my own, in her neck.

Suddenly, Payton's song couldn't end quickly enough. And, I rationalized, I'd already heard his band play.

Payton played the final notes. I lifted my fingers to my mouth to whistle. Jordan let go of my arm to clap, too, but I couldn't have that.

While Payton's bandmates made their way on stage, I turned to Jordan and grabbed her hips. Her eyes snapped up to mine, then widened. I watched carefully as they flared with the same emotions roiling through me, and I knew she wouldn't be upset with me for what I was about to do.

CHAPTER EIGHTEEN

Jordan

Asher took hold of my hips and gently pushed me toward the exit. The auditorium lights were dim, the empty vestibule lit only by the light coming from the hall.

He led me to a dark corner. Stacks of chairs lined the wall creating the perfect hiding place.

Asher didn't waste any time. As soon as we were hidden from view, his lips crushed mine.

Finally.

It had been too long. We had a lot to discuss, but that could wait. I missed him. I missed this. I wanted his kiss more than anything.

My arms twined around his neck as he dragged my body closer to his.

"It's you," he said between kisses. "Just you."

"I know." And I did. I believed him. After Payton told me how miserable Asher had been, I decided I'd been wrong. Judged him harshly. How could he kiss me like this and then want someone else? He couldn't. I didn't believe it.

Asher pulled back enough to look into my eyes.

"You know?"

I nodded. "I'm sorry I didn't listen. I'm sorry I didn't believe in you." I glanced down at the buttons on his shirt. "It had more to do with my insecurities than not knowing you wouldn't hurt me like that."

His breath came out a sharp sigh. "Jordan, I would never hurt you. Never on purpose, anyway." His hands framed my face. "I've never felt about anyone the way I feel about you." He kissed me softly, demanding, and he ended it all too soon. "I'm sorry, too, though. That night at the park, I've been thinking about how hard it would be for me if it was you, a million guys screaming your name. I would hate that. But I'm not going to stop singing or performing. All I can promise is to be respectful of you and my fans... and we have some. Jarom set up social media for us, and it's exploded."

"Seriously?" I had no idea how to feel about that, but I appreciated Asher's willingness to see things from my perspective. I'd never want him to give up his dream for me just like I'd never want to have to choose between him, or any guy, and hockey.

Asher nodded, and I knew right then, he was someone special. There were big things in store for this beautiful boy I'd fallen so hard for.

"If this is going to work..." I paused to gather my courage. "If this is going to work, we have to promise each other to be honest. To talk things out. And I promise not to shut you out, to listen." I'd learned a lot over the last couple of weeks, valuable lessons I hoped I never forgot. I had to respect Asher enough to hear his side of things and not jump to conclusions. We could have avoided a lot of heartache otherwise.

Asher kissed me again and tears pricked my eyes. "So, we're doing this? We're giving this another shot?"

I nodded. "Yes. I want to."

"I do, too. I've missed you so much, Jord."

This time I rose onto my toes to press my lips to his. We spent the next forty-five minutes behind that stack of chairs in the dim vestibule of the middle school auditorium. We might have stayed there longer if the lights hadn't come on and people hadn't come streaming out the doors.

Asher grinned and took my hand. "Come on, let's go congratulate Payton."

We threaded our way through the crowd mingling in the middle school commons until we found Payton accepting praise from my parents.

"I'm so proud of you," Mom said as she hugged Payton tight.

Payton's cheeks burned. "Thanks, Mom."

Dad slapped his back. "You did great, Pay. I had no idea you could sing like that."

"Yeah, what the heck? That was incredible." I only felt slightly guilty for missing him and his friends perform. At least I'd heard his solo.

Payton's eyes widened at the sight of Asher and me together. He immediately glanced down at our clasped hands and grinned. "It's about time."

At his words, both Mom and Dad turned to Asher and me.

Asher held out his hand to my mom. "Hi, Mrs. Parks. It's good to see you again."

Mom grinned, her elbow coming in contact with Dad's abdomen. "I like him. And call me Patricia."

Dad frowned. "Mrs. Parks will do just fine, son."

Asher stood up straight. "Yes, sir."

Mom rolled her eyes, her smile growing by the second. "I keep thinking we should have your folks over for dinner since we're neighbors and all. You'll have to give me your mom's number so we can chat."

Oh, dear. Asher's face paled, but he kept it together like a trooper. "Yes, ma'am."

It was time to intervene before he lost it. "Okay, well, I'm going to catch a ride home with Asher. Is that okay?" I directed my question to him, but my dad answered.

"That's fine, but not too late, Jordan."

Asher squeezed my hand.

"See you guys later. Good job, Pay."

Payton saluted, grinning as he watched Asher and me make our way to the exit.

"Where to?" Asher asked once we made it to his car.

I gave him a shy look through my lashes that made him smile.

"You got it."

Asher

We spent several hours in the space between our backyards. I hauled out a couple of blankets and held her close to keep her warm. We talked about what we both wanted, how we felt, and we kissed. A lot.

"I need to ask you something." Since we hadn't talked for a while, I hadn't had a chance to tell her about the concert or to ask if she wanted to go. I had a feeling I knew what her answer would be, but I had to make sure.

"Hmm. Sounds ominous." She lay tucked up against my side, her head resting on my chest, the blanket covering most of her face. It was too cold to be outside, but we didn't care.

"Not ominous. I made a deal with Payton a while back. If he did the talent show and didn't act like a jerk during mentoring, I'd take him to a concert."

Jordan lifted her head so she could see my face. "A concert? Why would you do that? Tickets are expensive."

I shook my head. "I have some I got for free."

She lifted a brow. "To see who?" I could tell she probably thought they were for some old geezer band at a dinner show or something.

"Carly Ryan."

Jordan sat up, shifting the blankets and letting cold air swirl around us. "Carly Ryan! How on earth did you get Carly Ryan tickets? I heard they sold out the first day they went on sale. For the whole tour!"

I sat up, too, and wrapped one of the blankets around both our shoulders. "They did."

Jordan stared at me, questions brewing in her eyes. "You said they were free. How did you get three free tickets to a sold-out show? Did you win them?"

I shook my head. The truth was coming to her, but she didn't want to believe it. Or couldn't.

"Tell me."

"You know. Think about it. You already know."

She sagged. "Are you serious?"

"I get free tickets to every show. Even the ones on the other side of the world."

Jordan wiped her hand across her forehead. "Wow. I can't believe it." She reached for my hands. "Carly Ryan is your mom?"

I didn't say anything, just lifted my brows in a 'what can you do' kind of way.

"Wow," she said again. For a few seconds she didn't say anything and then she looked at me and frowned. "All that stuff you told me... You don't see her? The checks on National Rubber Duckie Day?" She touched my cheek. "That's gotta be hard."

I turned my face into her palm. "It's not. I don't remember anything ever being different than it is right now. I don't hate her. I don't blame her. In her way, I know she loves me."

"Does anybody know? Nobody knows?" She shook her head with disbelief.

"People know. She hasn't hidden me. You could Google her. I show up as her kid on wiki sites. All my friends back in Minnesota know. But I'm not around her much and never in public. There aren't many pictures of us together." The only one I'd ever seen on the internet was taken when I was about ten. You couldn't even see my face. She was hugging me after one of her concerts, the only one my dad ever took me to. She'd talked about me in interviews. I tried not to watch them. It made her sad to talk about me. I knew she had regrets. It was easier to forgive her if I didn't dwell on it.

"I can't wrap my head around it."

I watched her carefully. It always felt like a gamble, letting people in. Would Jordan act differently around me now she knew? Would she expect things from me? My mom might be rich and famous, but that didn't mean I had access to her wealth or fame. And I didn't want to.

Sure, if I needed something, I knew she'd come through. But I didn't call her up asking for things all the time.

"It's cool. Thank you for inviting me to the concert. I'm sure we'll have fun."

That was it? I wrapped my arms around her and pulled the blanket more securely around us. "You're not all weirded out?"

Jordan shook her head. "Nope. I mean, wow. But she isn't a part of your life." She leaned against me, laying her ear against my chest over my heart. "Knowing who your mom is doesn't change who you are. And I'm more interested in you."

"Oh, really?" I asked, rolling onto my back and pulling her with me.

"Really," Jordan giggled.

"What exactly are you interested in?"

Jordan's eyes sparkled in the soft light from the moon. "I'm interested in this." She kissed my chin. "And this." Her lips grazed my jaw. "And this." She reached for my cheek, but I turned my head, so she kissed my lips instead. She giggled against them, but only for a moment before I deepened the kiss.

Forget falling. I'd already fallen.

EPILOGUE

Jordan

Just before graduation...

Asher: Where are you?
    Me: Calm down. We're almost there.
    Asher: I can't see you.
    Me: There are twenty thousand people here!
    Asher: Just hurry. I need to see you. I swear I'm going to throw up.
    Me: I'm coming, babe. Just breathe.

I could picture Asher pacing backstage. Jarom and the other guys never seemed to get as nervous for some reason, but Asher turned into a complete basket case just before walking on stage. Of course, this show would be unlike anything Breakout had ever done before. Tonight was their first night opening for Carly Ryan on her new tour.

As Carly's security guys carved a path for me to the seat reserved for me, front and center of the stage, I thought back to the night when Asher made good on his promise to Payton and took us to see Carly's concert. We'd collected our tickets at will call, and almost immediately, Carly's assistant, Amanda, appeared out of nowhere and ushered us backstage where we met Payton's favorite band, Carbine. We spent about ten starstruck minutes talking to Carbine before their set started. Once they left to go onstage, Amanda escorted us to Carly's dressing room.

Asher hugged his mom, his clammy hand still gripping mine. He wouldn't let me go. He acted tough, but seeing her wasn't as easy for him as he let on.

Carly hadn't at all been what I expected. From the way Asher described her from those early days, I thought she might be aloof, distracted. But she was warm, welcoming, and thrilled to see Asher. Her eyes lit the moment he walked into her dressing room, and she couldn't seem to stop touching him. Caressing his shoulder. Brushing his hair from his forehead. She must have hugged him ten times in the twenty minutes we visited with her.

He was right.

She did love him.

So did his dad. After the concert, Asher began seeing more and more of his mom. She took an interest in his songwriting and even sang a couple of his songs on her last album. Derek hadn't been very excited about Asher's plans but recognized a losing battle when he saw one. Asher would never play hockey the way his dad wanted him to, and he'd just had to accept that. Shari helped.

"Here you are, Miss Parks," one of the security guards gestured toward a roped-off section beside the sound guys with a single padded chair. I'd invited Natalie and Kelly, but neither of them could get away.

"Thanks, guys." I climbed over the ropes into my secluded area. It wasn't very big and not as conspicuous as it felt.

"We'll be back as soon as Mr. Sloane is finished to take you back to him." Asher worried about me getting trampled or something, I guess.

I thought the security and special seating arrangement were overkill, but Asher insisted.

I nodded to the security guards as I pulled my phone back out of my pocket. Two more texts from Asher. Surely, he should be concentrating on what he was about to do! Still, I was the same way before every hockey game. I'd be playing for the University of Wisconsin. Asher wouldn't always make it to my games, but I knew he'd try.

Me: I'm here. Can you see me?

My hand shot up in the air.

Asher: Yes. Can you see me?

I scanned the left side of the stage, where I knew he would be. He stood in the shadows, but I'd recognize that silhouette anywhere.

Me: Yes, babe. You're going to be amazing.

Asher: I love you.

My heart leaped in my chest. He'd said the words before, many times, but it didn't matter. Each time felt like the first.

Me: I love you, too. Knock em dead.

I looked back up, and Jarom, Adam, and Bash had already found their places onstage. I marveled that Asher could send me a text message one second and stride out in front of thousands of screaming fans the next. But that's just what he did.

Who needed a padded chair? I couldn't sit down if my legs fell off. With my heart in my throat, I watched Asher point out into the audience, right to me. Our eyes connected.

"This is for you, baby," his silky voice said into his microphone. "Always for you."

———

HOW ABOUT SOME DIVAS!
COMING June/July 2020!
THE DANGERS OF DATING A DIVA

Book One, Kissing the Player by Maggie Dallen
Book Two, Kissing the Hero by Christina Benjamin

Book Three, Kissing the Debutant by Michelle Macqueen and Ann Maree Craven
Book Four, Kissing the Shy Guy by Stephanie Street

WANT MORE TOMBOYS?

Grab Book 3, Playing the Field by Christina Benjamin HERE
Keep reading for a sneak peek

And if you missed Book 1, Playing the Enemy by Maggie Dallen, grab
your copy HERE

JOIN THE NEWSLETTER

Want to hear about all of Stephanie Street's new releases plus other great deals from other authors? Sign up for her newsletter today for amazing deals and giveaways.

PLUS a free novella, Us at the Beach

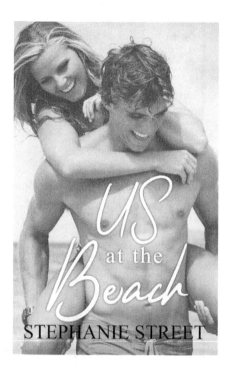

GET MY FREE NOVELLA

PLAYING THE FIELD

By Christina Benjamin

Prologue
Alex's Story

I don't know how to describe my first kiss to you. I also don't know if it was so incredibly mind-blowingly magical because the lips to first touch mine belonged to Grant King, but I'm not going to dwell on that. I'm going to dwell on how we finally got there. Because this play took some extra innings.

Chapter 1
Alex

"What do you mean there's no softball team?" I demanded, my hands instantly balling into fists.

"Calm down, sweetie," my mom said, brushing off my outrage like she hadn't just dropped a bomb on me. "Your dad will put a call into the school. We'll get this sorted out."

"Mom!" I exclaimed. "Softball is my life! I'm a junior this year. If I don't play softball my chances to get an athletic scholarship will be nonexistent!"

"I know, sweetheart. No need to be so dramatic. We'll sort something out for you."

I bit my nails as I glared out the car window. I hated when my mom talked about my future in sports like it was no more pressing than her grocery list. She probably thought she could swap items out just as easily as replacing Double Stuf Oreos for chocolate chip cookies. *'No softball at your new school, sweetie? No problem. We'll just swap it out for scrapbook club.'*

Why didn't she understand, for some things in life, there were no substitutions?

My mom would never dare treat my brothers this way. But then again everything in life was easier for boys, wasn't it?

I was still trying to absorb the bitter reality my mom had just served as my new high school came into view. The unimpressive brick building was barely visible between the lush, green pine trees. It was a stark difference from my last school in Arizona, and the one before that in California. Before that was New York, then Massachusetts, then California again, then Nevada, then . . .

Honestly, it's too exhausting to recount.

To say I was used to starting over was an understatement. Each year brought a new school, a new start, a new team. That's the deal when your dad is David Prince, retired MLB legend turned college baseball coach. He had to go where the jobs were and we had to go with him.

Well, not all of us.

Not anymore.

This was the first time I'd be starting at a new school alone. I was used to having my brothers with me to help ease the transition. But as of last year, I'm the last of the Prince kids without a high school diploma.

Sometimes being the youngest is the worst. Actually, it's always the worst.

I love my family don't get me wrong, but there are a few things you probably need to know to understand where I'm coming from.

First of all, I'm the youngest of five children. All of them boys.

Except me of course. The funny thing is, I was supposed to be a boy. Or at least that's what the doctors thought.

How they could get something like that wrong in this day and age is beyond me, but it's just my luck that they did.

My parents were expecting baby number five to be another bouncing baby boy. One more to add to the Prince brood of blue-eyed boys; Sam, Zach, Luke and Will. But what they got was a big old surprise.

Me.

The crazy thing is . . . sometimes I think my life would be a heck of a lot easier if I'd just been born the boy everyone was expecting. Because being a tomboy isn't easy.

By the time I was born my name had already been painted on my blue nursery wall and printed on my token Prince infant-sized baseball jersey. Luckily, my parents picked a name a girl could rock—Alex.

That's me—Alex Prince.

Actually, my name is one of my favorite things about me. It has swagger. It's probably the best thing to come out of my doctor's gender blunder. If my mom had known she was having a baby girl, she would've named me something ridiculous like Rosebud or Petunia. As it was, she'd made my dad repaint my room pink, and traded out all my practical baby boy clothes for frilly things made of ruffles and lace.

I get it. I really do. My mom had been an army of one in a house of testosterone for a long time. When I came along, she thought she was finally getting reinforcements. The trouble was, she got me, a total tomboy.

By the time I could walk she knew she could kiss her ideas of pedicures and princess parties goodbye. My idea of dress-up was putting on my dad's old baseball jersey and playing catch with the boys.

At sixteen, not much has changed.

My mom still desperately decorated every new bedroom of mine in powdery pink pastels and I still wore baseball hand-me-downs and played catch with boys. But now, I wasn't toddling after them—more like running circles around them.

The truth was, I was a good athlete. More than good. Thanks to the tough love of my brothers and tutelage of my dad, I could outplay just about anyone who stepped foot on a baseball field with me—male or female.

But if the sinking feeling in my chest was any indicator, I wouldn't be doing any of that at this new softball-less school of mine.

I wasn't sure how my dad was going to pull a softball team out of thin air, but he'd never let me down before. He didn't seem as bothered as my mom that his daughter had turned out to be a tomboy. I decided not to waste time dwelling on my current sports dilemma. I had other things to worry about. Like not being pegged as the weird new girl.

Here goes nothing!

Playing the Field releases on November 13!

ALSO BY STEPHANIE STREET

<u>Young Adult Romance</u>

Don't Pretend You Love Me

Book 1 of the Just Don't Romance series

Don't Forget About Me

Book 2 of the Just Don't Romance series

Don't Kiss Me Breathless

Book 3 of the Just Don't Romance series

Don't Leave Me Behind

Book 4 of the Just Don't Romance series

Dating: One on One

Book 1 of the Eastridge Heights Basketball series

Dating: On the Rebound

Book 2 of the Eastridge Heights Basketball series

Dating: For the Block

Book 3 of the Eastridge Heights Basketball series

Dating: For the Assist

Book 4 of the Eastridge Heights Basketball series

Save Me

A Stand Alone Clean Romance

Us at the Beach

A Stand Alone Clean Romance

Playing to Win

Book 2 of the Trouble with Tomboys series

Road Trip With a Nerd

A Stand Alone Clean Romance Novella

Clean Billionaire Romance

Marrying the Football Billionaire

Book 1 in the Marrying the Celebrity Billionaire series

Humbling the Spoiled Billionaire

Book 2 in the Marrying the Celebrity Billionaire series

Contemporary Romance

Chasing Paris

A Stand Alone Clean Romance

FIND STEPHANIE STREET

Stephanie Street - Author Instagram Feed
Stephanie Street - Facebook Page

Email Address:
stephaniestreetauthor@gmail.com

Website -
www.stephaniestreetauthor.com

Join my Street Team on Facebook
https://www.facebook.com/groups/Authorstephaniestreetscreamteam/